## Praise for Ben Arzate

"There is a group of fresh voices taking weirdness very seriously, and Ben Arzate is one of its leading figures. *The Story of the Y* is a mysterious, adventurous hybrid. This is the love child of Carlos Fuentes and Hunter S. Thompson, covered in blood and desert dust, screaming outside a Mexican restaurant. Listen to it."
　　　　　　—Gabino Iglesias, author of *Coyote Songs*

"A wild road trip to Mexico with more turns than a long line at the bank. Arzate's prose flashes like a switchblade."
　　　　　　—Bram Riddlebarger, author of *Golden Rod*

"What starts off as a seemingly quiet story about a mysterious record quickly turns into a bizarre and violent ride across a Mexican landscape imbued with Mr. Arzate's unique brand of humor and sense of surrealism. If Robert Rodriguez and Barry Gifford worked in the bizarro genre this would be the outcome. A wicked fun read!"
　　　　　　—Philip LoPresti, author of *A God Of Flies Among Them*

THE STORY OF THE Y

BEN ARZATE

CABAL BOOKS

THE STORY OF THE Y

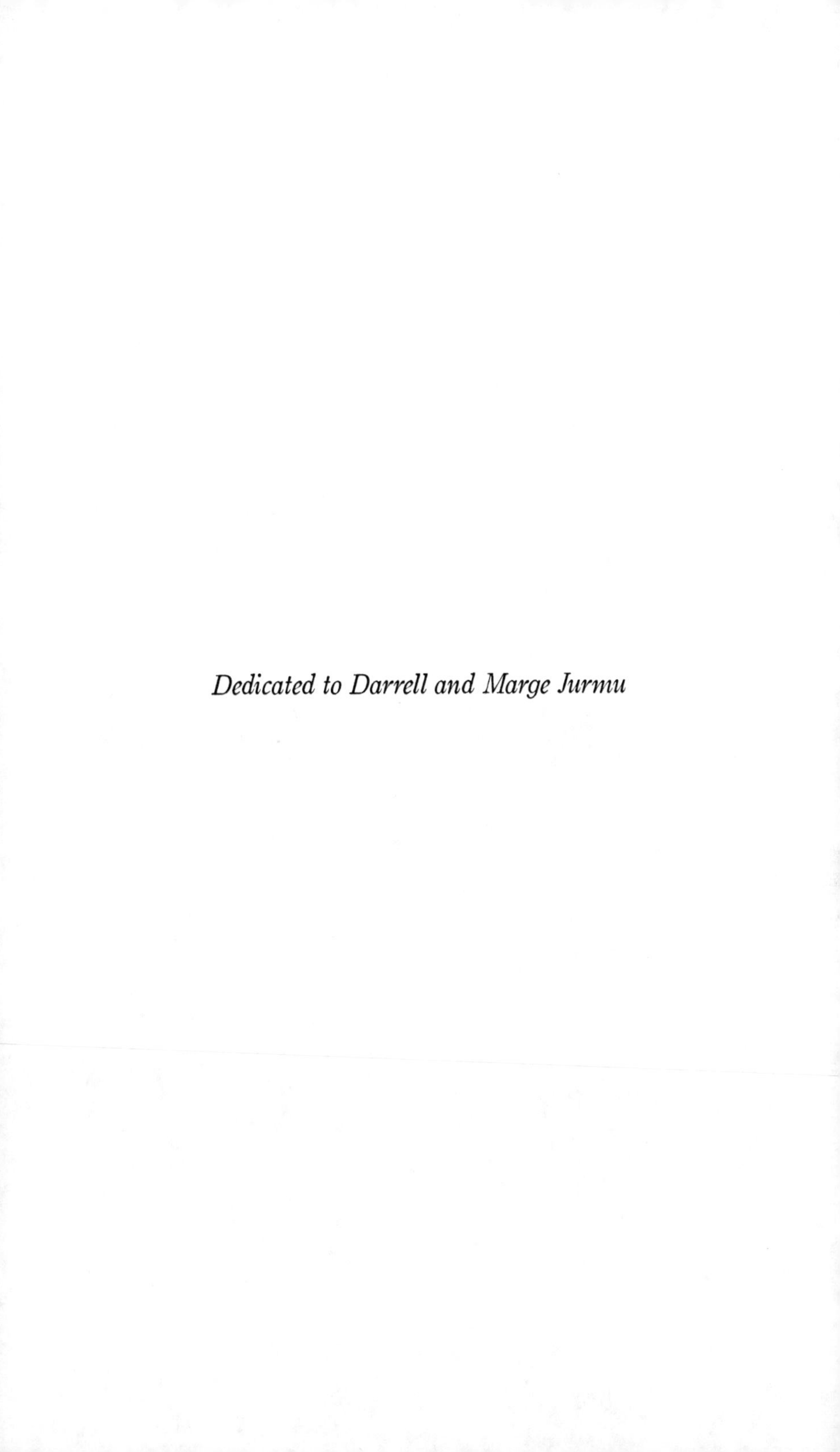

*Dedicated to Darrell and Marge Jurmu*

Writing about music is like dancing about architecture.
QUOTE OF UNKNOWN ORIGIN


"You're spiraling into an abyss of dementia."
IRWIN CHUSID, in response to a self-proclaimed
obsessed Y. Bhekhirst fan


The passion for destruction is a creative passion, too!
MIKHAIL BAKUNIN, *The Reaction in Germany*

Thank you very much for picking up *The Story of the Y*.

One thing I should let you know is that Y. Bhekhirst, the subject of this novel, is not a product of my imagination. The real Y. Bhekhirst is, or maybe was, a rock musician of whom very little is known about to this day. No known photographs, interviews, or anything besides their music and copyright records exist.

Y. Bhekhirst released an album and a single independently, both called *Hot in the Airport*, to several music stores in New York City in 1986. They never released anything else as far as anyone knows. Almost no one paid attention to these releases until music journalist and radio DJ Irwin Chusid began playing them on his show on WFMU in the mid-90's. Since then, they've become known among fans of what is usually called "outsider music,"

music whose strangeness often comes from the naivete of the artist rather than intentional experimentation.

The songs of *Hot in the Airport* are difficult to categorize. Others have described them as "post-punk," "experimental rock," and "free jazz." Since no interviews or statements from Y. Bhekhirst themselves exist, it's unknown whether they set out to make a strange album or whether they stumbled into it by accident while attempting to make something more straightforward. Whatever the songs are, I found them inspiring enough to write the book you're now holding.

The Y. Bhekhirst of this novel is loosely based on the scant facts that exist about them, but they are a heavily fictionalized version. When you finish this book, I hope you'll feel compelled to seek out the music of the real Y. Bhekhirst.

Without further ado, please enjoy *The Story of the Y*.

BEN ARZATE

*Track 1*

"Is he saying 'go slow today' or 'no snow today'?" Alex says.

He sits on the floor listening to a cassette tape on a boom box. Next to him is a portable turntable. A record with the title *Reachin'* and the artist name Arcesia is playing on the turntable. The needle is on the label. A crackling comes out of the speaker. A voice speaks over the crackling.

"I think he's saying 'go slow,'" the voice says. "That jives with the 'speed 45' line."

"I could swear I'm hearing 'no snow'," Alex says. "That doesn't seem to follow though. Why would you run your car that slow if there's no snow?"

"Maybe he's saying both, you dig? Maybe that's his bag, driving safe even in fair weather."

"That's stupid."

"This whole album is stupid, man. Why are we listening to it?"

"You're one to talk, John."

Alex reaches over. He stops the cassette. He picks up the case. He examines it. It is yellow with the letters "HDG" in light blue. The text reads *Hot in the Airport* and underneath "Singer: Y. Bhekhirst".

"It is a pretty interesting listen, even if it is stupid," Alex says. "It's like someone not really right in the head making a sincere attempt at pop music."

"That describes most of what you listen to," John says.

"Hey, you know that includes you."

"I'm right in the head."

"Well, I doubt you're trapped in that record because you were normal."

"If I'm being punished because someone thought I was some crazy burn-out, it's not my fault."

Alex reaches over. He hits PLAY on the boom box. The next song begins. Alex looks at the cassette case.

"'Rain in Summer,'" Alex says. "This guy's even more obsessed with weather than you."

•

Alex walks into Snoring Records. He walks up to the counter.

"Hey, what's up Chris?" he says to the cashier.

"Hey, Alex," Chris says.

"Got anything new I might like?"

"Take a look for yourself. I never know what your weird ass is going to like."

"Oh, thanks a lot. This isn't *High Fidelity*. Show your customers some respect."

"Well, it's not like you don't come back after I bust your balls."

"Whatever, man. Do you have any more haunted records?"

"If you find any, take them. I don't want to be babysitting any more ghosts."

"John's not a bad roommate."

"Are you kidding? He can't even pay rent."

"Yeah, but I got a good interview out of him."

"Well, take a look around. Your article about him did make good advertising. When it first came out anyway."

Alex walks over to new records. He looks through them. He picks up a compilation of early 20th century classical music. He looks through the country records. He picks up a Charley Pride album. He looks through the jazz records. He picks up an Al Hirt album. He looks through the rock records. He picks up a compilation of rockabilly songs. He looks through the singles. He picks up one in a white sleeve. He looks at the label. The artist is Y. Bhekhirst and the song is titled "Hot in the Airport." He takes the records to the counter. Chris begins to ring them up.

"Y. Bekurs?" Chris says. "Didn't you buy a tape of this guy here a little while ago?"

"Bhekhirst," Alex says. "Yeah. He's pretty weird, but I like him."

Chris looks at both sides of the record's label.

"Huh, same song on both sides," he says. "That's pointless. He really couldn't find a song for the B-side?"

"Guess not."

"Is this song on that tape?"

"Yeah. But this is supposed to be really hard to find and you're only charging a dollar for it."

"Well, I don't know. This was in a big box that a lady sold me for, like, ten bucks. I couldn't find anything on how much this damn record is actually worth, so I figured it was junk."

"It is, so please give it to me for only a dollar."

"Whatever."

Chris finishes ringing up the records.

"$31.13 in total," he says.

"Do I have any store credit left?"

"Only like a quarter's worth."

"Okay, here's $40. Put the change towards my credit."

"All right. Here's your stuff. Have a good day."

"Thanks. See ya."

•

Alex walks into his apartment. He sets the bag of records on his couch. He walks over to the portable turntable. He turns it on. The record on it spins.

"Hey, John," Alex says.

"Hey, man. Score anything good at the record store?" John says from the turntable speaker.

"I got something pretty interesting,"

Alex takes the "Hot in the Airport" record from the bag.

"You know that Bhekhirst album I showed you the other day? I found the single from it."

Alex pulls the record from the sleeve. An envelope falls to the floor. Alex picks it up. He opens the flap.

"What's that?" John says.

"I don't know. It looks like a letter."

Alex takes the letter from the envelope. He opens it. It is written in Spanish. Alex takes a picture with his phone. He selects "Primavera" from his contacts. He sends it.

*"Hey, babe. What does this letter say? I found it in a record I bought."*

Alex studies the envelope.

"The return address is in Mexico City," he says. "Looks like it was addressed to someone named Elizabeth Charrington here in Monk City."

"Who does it say sent it?"

"It says it's from a Pepe Díaz."

Alex's phone beeps. He looks at the screen. Primavera has sent a text.

*"Hey bebé. Give me a sec and I'll email you what it says."*

"The hand writing on this is really nice," Alex says. "I don't see a date or anything on it. I wonder how old it is?"

"What's the postmark say?" John says.

Alex checks the envelope.

"Looks like June of 1999. It's kind of faded though."

Alex's phone beeps. He checks it. Primavera has sent an email.

"Here's what the letter says,

*'My lovely Elizabeth,*

*I hope this package finds you well. It took me some time to find a copy of this record. Not many were made in the first place. I can't say I fully stand behind the song, but I enjoyed making it. It was certainly an experience. I will try to find a copy of the album that we put together. I don't seem to have any among my personal belongings. I'll write to my colleague and ask if they have any.*

*Yours Truly,*

*Pepe Díaz'"*

•

Alex sits at a table in Pagan Coffee. Across from him is Larry. Larry wears an ill-fitting suit. His left hand resembles a lobster claw.

"I went to the address on the envelope and it looks like nobody has lived there for a while. The house was in pretty bad shape. I can't find anything on the Elizabeth woman," Alex says.

Larry reaches in his jacket with his claw hand. He pulls out a flask. He pours some of the liquor into his coffee cup.

"So, you just want to run down to Mexico and find the guy? What if that place is abandoned too?"

"Lobster, I'm telling you, if I can interview this Pepe guy, it'll be a huge piece. I'll get enough attention to finally write about music full time. This Pepe Diaz is listed on the copyright for the album. My guess is Pepe Diaz is Y. Bhekhirst. I think it's worth the risk. The worst that happens is we waste a few days."

Larry holds out the flask to Alex. Alex holds his cup out. Larry pours some of the liquor into it.

"You said that about finding that ghost in the record and you're still working at the bank," Larry says. "You had to self-publish your last few articles on your blog."

"I still made a lot of money off that interview. I just didn't capitalize on it when I could have."

Alex sips his coffee. The liquor hits his throat. He scrunches his face. He shakes his head.

"Capitalize on it how?" Larry says. "You think *Twisting* would publish your article about albums that are just fucking wind noises?"

"If I had enough clout, then yeah, I could publish an article about Arctic Ambient music in a big-time outlet. Maybe not *Twisting* but definitely a place like *Tuning Fork*. Nobody knows who the hell Y. Bhekhirst is. If I can uncover his identity and interview him, it'll be a really big deal."

"So why do you need me to drive you? Why don't you just take a bus?"

"It'll be way better if we have a car. Plus, you're more familiar with Mexico."

"I only ever go down there to get weed and pills. It's cheaper down there. Plus, it's not like I like going down there. It's dirty and most of the people are assholes."

"Look, I'll pay you back for all the gas and any other expense. Primavera's down to go, so why not? It'll be like a vacation."

"Fine. I could use some more weed anyway."

"So, it's settled then. In two weeks, we head off to Mexico to find Y. Bhekhirst."

Larry raises his coffee cup.

"To Mexico!"

Alex raises his coffee cup.

"To Mexico, my friend!"

Alex and Larry sip from their cups. Alex clenches his teeth to keep from shaking his head again.

•

Larry drives the car. Alex and Primavera are in the backseat. Alex holds the portable turntable in his lap. The Arcesia record is on the turntable. Primavera listens to a Walkman. She turns off the Walkman. She takes off the headphones.

"These Y. Bhekhirst songs are really weird, and kind of creepy. Do you know anything about him?" Primavera says.

She takes the cassette out of the Walkman. She hands the cassette to Alex.

Alex takes the cassette. He puts the cassette in the case. He puts the case in his backpack on the floor.

"There's barely any information on him at all. Back in the late 80's and early 90's, he apparently dropped his albums off in record stores in New York City. No one knows anything else. I was able to find his name in the U.S. Copyright Office records. Apparently, Y. Bhekhirst is one of several names listed with his songs. Pepe Díaz is also one of them, so it has to be his real name. He must have made a lot more songs. There were a bunch listed that aren't on the tape. I found an address in Queens, New York too. I called there, but it looks like someone unrelated to him lives there now."

"Maybe he left because he was a serial killer or something. His songs sound like he had problems," Primavera says.

"Well, maybe he did. I think he just really wanted to make music, but didn't bother to learn his instruments beyond the very basics."

"Like how you did?" Larry says.

"Shut up. I was in high school when I made those songs. Besides, I can play piano way better now."

"You still can't sing."

Alex ignores Larry.

"Anyway, based on how he talked to that Elizabeth woman in the letter, he sounds like he's really nice. Maybe kind of old fashioned."

"How do you think he knew that Elizabeth chick?" John says. "You think she was his old lady?"

"No idea," Alex says. "I'll just have to ask him when we find him."

•

Larry's car enters a border checkpoint. He pulls into the "nothing to declare" route. The light in the lane turns red.

"Ah, shit," Larry says.

He pulls into the inspection lane.

Primavera shifts in her seat.

"I really don't like Border Patrol," she says. "My cousin got harassed pretty badly by them when she went to Mexico."

"I don't like them either, babe," Alex says. "Let's just cooperate with them so we can get this over with."

Two Border Patrol guards walk up to Larry's window. One guard is bald. He has a scar on his face. The other guard wears sunglasses. He has a goatee. Larry rolls down the window.

"Is there a problem?" Larry says.

The bald guard looks in the backseat.

"Why do you have a record player?" he says

"This is the only way I can talk to them," John says from the turntable.

The bald guard scrunches his face. The sunglasses-wearing guard sighs.

"Could all of you step out of the car?" the bald guard says.

"Are we being detained?" Alex says.

"Are we being detained?" the sunglasses-wearing guard says in a mocking tone. "Yes, you're being fucking detained. Now get out of the fucking car, and bring that fucking record with you."

Larry, Alex, and Primavera sit in a holding room. The bald guard looks at a tablet. The sunglasses-wearing guard examines the Arcesia record.

"Do you mind telling me why three Mexicans are taking a ghost into Mexico?" The bald guard says.

"Mexican? I'm Cuban," Larry says.

"And I'm Spanish," Primavera says.

"I'm only half Mexican, and I was born in the States," Alex says.

"Same fucking thing," the sunglasses-wearing guard says. "'Ar-sees-aye-ah,' the ghost is on a Mexican record, too."

"He's Italian," Alex says.

"Same! Fucking! Thing!" the sunglasses-wearing guard says. "Why do you have this fucking ghost and why the fuck are you taking it to Mexico?"

"I'm a music journalist, and I'm going to Mexico to interview a musician," Alex says. "I'm bringing John because he's a friend."

"Friends with a ghost," the bald guard says.

He shakes his head.

"Only a fucking Mexican," the sunglasses-wearing guard says. "Do you know how much we've had to deal with you people bringing ghosts across the fucking border? Do you know what the fucking things do when they get over here? Did you not read about that lady with a fucking Mexican ghost that got in her house? It was spying on her when she was fucking showering. She was so fucking scared that she fell over and nearly cracked her head on the fucking toilet. I'm fucking sick of you people jumping over the border with your fucking ghosts."

"They're becoming a bigger problem than illegal immigrants," the bald guard says.

"I haven't heard anything about that," Primavera says.

"Then read the fucking news," the sunglasses-wearing guard says.

"I read the news every day."

"Then read it in fucking English. En een-gleesh, comprendo?"

"What the fuck is your deal?" Alex says.

"Watch your mouth, young man," the bald guard says.

Larry elbows Alex. "Keep your mouth shut."

"Listen to your freak friend with the fucked-up hand, asshole," the sunglasses-wearing guard says.

"Hey, fuck you!" Larry says.

The sunglasses-wearing guard slaps Larry with the Arcesia record.

"You ain't fucking pretty enough for me!" the sunglasses-wearing guard says.

"Dude, don't do that!" Alex says. "I have no idea what will happen if you break that!"

"Is that fucking right?" the sunglasses-wearing guard says. "Let's just see what happens then."

The sunglasses-wearing guard starts to bend the Arcesia record.

"Shit!" Alex says.

He dives forward. He swings his fist. He hits the sunglasses-wearing guard in the groin. The sunglasses-wearing guard drops the record. He grabs his groin. He falls to the ground. He vomits. He shakes. He cries.

"Stop!" the bald guard says.

He tackles Alex. He pins Alex to the ground. Larry jumps up. He grabs the bald guard by the neck with his claw hand. He squeezes. The bald guard chokes. He jumps up. He falls back on Larry. Larry keeps a grip on the bald guard's neck. Primavera stands up. She helps Alex up. The bald guard reaches for his gun. Alex steps on the bald guard's arm. Larry keeps squeezing the bald guard's neck. The bald guard goes limp.

"You motherfuckers!" the sunglasses-wearing guard says.

He tries to stand up. He vomits again. He falls back on the floor into his vomit.

Primavera grabs the Arcesia record.

"Let's go!" she says.

Larry, Alex, and Primavera run out of the holding room. They run out of the Border Patrol building. They run to Larry's car. Larry jumps in the driver seat. Alex and Primavera jump in the back. Larry starts the car. He steps on the gas. The car lurches forward. A barrier arm ahead is down. Larry steps harder on the gas. The car breaks through the barrier arm.

•

Larry slows the car down. He looks in the rear-view mirror. He can't see the border anymore.

"Holy shit!" Larry says. "I've dealt with some asshole border guards, but those guys were fucking psychos!"

"No kidding," Alex says.

"I was so scared," Primavera says.

Alex hugs Primavera.

"I was too, baby," he says.

"You must have hit that guy's nuts pretty damn hard to make him stay down. Where'd you learn to punch like that?" Larry says.

"I guess I don't know my own strength," Alex says.

"You didn't kill that guard, did you, Lobster?" Primavera says.

"No, I just made him pass out."

"How do you know?"

"Believe me, I know."

"Pri, can you hand me the record?" Alex says. "I want to make sure John's all right."

Primavera grabs the Arcesia record. Alex picks up the turntable. Primavera puts the record on the turntable. She puts the needle on the label.

"John," Alex says, "is everything okay?"

"Yeah. I'm groovy, man." John says. "Thanks for saving my ass."

"What would happen if the record broke?" Alex says.

"I have no idea, honestly. It might leave me trapped here forever without being able to talk to anyone. It might make me disintegrate altogether. That'd be a drag. Maybe it would do something good, like free me, but I don't want to take the risk."

"Good thing we stopped him then."

"You want to get out of that record, John?" Primavera says.

"More than anything," John says.

"That guard said there were a lot of ghosts coming from Mexico. So there's got to be some people who know a lot about ghosts down here. Maybe we can find someone who knows how to get you out of there."

"That's a good idea. We'll ask around," Alex says.

"Maybe he was just full of shit." Larry says. "He was out of his fucking mind."

"It's worth a try," Primavera says.

"So now we've got two goals; find Y. Bhekhirst and find a way to free John," Alex says.

"Three goals actually. I want to pick up some things while I'm down here," Larry says.

"What kind of things?" Primavera says.

"Just things," Larry says. "Don't worry about it, Pri. It won't take long."

"Far out! Thanks guys," John says.

•

The sun goes down. Larry pulls the car over to the side of the road. He looks at his phone. He looks at a map app. A coyote howls.

"I don't get it," Larry says. "I know that Alamo Azul is right around here. I always stop in it when I come down."

"Where's the nearest town from here?" Alex says.

"I don't know. The GPS on my phone is fucking up."

"We're still in the middle of the desert."

"I fucking know that, okay?"

"Don't get all mad at me, it's not my damn fault."

"Guys, don't fight," Primavera says.

Larry throws his phone on the front seat.

"Well, fuck it," he says. "There can't be anything around for miles and I'm way too tired. Let's just sleep here and figure it out in the morning."

"What if the Border Patrol finds us here?" Primavera says.

"We have to be a long way from the border by now," Larry says.

"We'll be fine, Pri," Alex says. "Let's just get some sleep. We'll get up early and try to figure out where we are."

The turntable is on the floor.

"I'm not ready to snooze yet. You mind if I sing you all to sleep?" John says.

"Sure, go ahead," Alex says.

"Can't we just listen to the radio?" Larry says.

"Just let him sing."

Larry stretches out across the front seats. Alex and Primavera spoon on the backseat. John sings "Blue Shadows" by Roy Rogers and the Sons of the Pioneers. Larry, Alex, and Primavera fall asleep. John stops singing. Snoring comes from the turntable.

Alex wakes up. He wakes up Primavera. Larry is still asleep.

"Hey, Larry, get up," Alex says.

Larry goes on sleeping.

Alex reaches into the front seat. He shakes Larry. Larry jolts up. He looks around.

"What the hell?" Larry says. "Oh, yeah. Fuck, that was a bad nightmare."

"Can we go?" Primavera says. "I really want to take a shower."

"Yeah, yeah," Larry says.

He picks up his phone. He looks at the map app.

"What the fuck? It says we should be right in the middle of Alamo Azul. Either the town just disappeared or the GPS is still fucked."

"Does it say that there's anything nearby?" Alex says.

"It says there's another town three hours up the road from here. But that can't be right."

"We may as well try. Where else can we go?" Alex says.

•

Larry's car pulls into a town. The sign by the road reads ATASCADEROS. Larry looks at his phone.

"Seriously, what the fuck? We're at Atascaderos like the GPS says, but Alamo Azul just wasn't there. Where the hell was it?"

"Are you sure that's where the town was?" John says.

"Yes. I'm not crazy. I've been there several times. I've stayed overnight there."

"You weren't drinking, were you?" Alex says.

"Well, yeah. But I wasn't that shit-faced and I was sober when I arrived. I'm telling you that fucking town was there. All 5,000 people couldn't have just moved and had everything disappear without a trace since I was there last goddamn year. Something had to have fucking happened."

"Calm down, Lobster. Maybe it was just your map app glitching out," Alex says. "Let's just stop and stay here for today. We can get our bearings and head off to Mexico City early tomorrow."

"Fine. There's a place just up ahead."

Larry pulls into the parking lot of a motel. The sign reads LA PIEDRA MOTEL Y RESTAURANTE. Larry parks. He gets out of the car. He comes back with two room keys. Alex and Primavera get out of the car. They get their bags out of the trunk. Primavera carries the turntable. They follow Larry to the rooms.

•

Larry sits on the bed of his room. Alex and Primavera sit on the floor. The turntable is next to Alex.

"I asked the guy at the desk if he knew what happened to Alamo Azul," Larry says. "He said that nobody knows. He said he had a brother living there. He tried to call him a month ago, and nobody answered. Just a message that the line wasn't in service. He called the cops to report his brother missing, but they couldn't find the town. It was gone without a trace. All the people there disappeared. All 5,000 of them. The Federales are investigating, but you know how they are down here; if they aren't corrupt, they're incompetent."

"You seem really bothered by it," Alex says.

"Hell yeah, I am. I knew people from there. I was friends with them. I was hoping I could stop there to get some of the shit I wanted."

"Sorry, Lobster."

Larry shakes his head.

"Forget it," he says. "I asked him how I could get to Mexico City from here, too. He didn't know, but I got a map off him. If my phone GPS craps out, we can use that. We should be there in another day or two."

"Did you ask him if he knew anything about ghosts?" John says.

"No, I didn't fucking ask him. Are you expecting me to do everything?"

"Come on, relax, Lobster," Alex says. "We'll go get some something to eat and a couple drinks. We need a little relaxation after what happened yesterday."

"Yeah, that sounds good. I need some fucking cerveza and tequila," Larry says.

•

Larry, Alex, and Primavera sit at a table in a restaurant. The waiter comes. He has no mouth. There is blank flesh under his nose. He takes their plates.

"Otra cerveza y tequila, por favor," Larry says to the waiter.

The waiter nods. The waiter brings Larry another Victoria beer and shot of Lunazul blanco tequila. Larry kills the tequila shot.

Larry looks around the restaurant. He looks at the bar.

"Hey, I need to go take care of something," he says. "I'll be right back."

Larry gets up. He walks to the bar. He talks to the bartender.

"What's he doing?" Primavera says.

"I don't know. You know how Lobster is. He's always got something going on," Alex says.

Larry comes back to the table.

"When we leave tomorrow, I need to stop somewhere just outside of town," he says.

"All right," Alex says.

"Where do you need to go?" Primavera says.

"Just some place to pick up the things I need."

"What things?"

"Just things."

"It's not drugs is it?"

"Look, don't worry about it, okay?"

Larry drinks his beer.

•

Primavera sits on the bed in the motel room. Alex is next to her.

"I'm really worried," Primavera says. "I think Lobster is up to something."

"He probably is," Alex says. "Has he ever caused us any harm though?"

"No, but we already had a problem with the Border Patrol. It's probably going to be hard to get back into America."

"We'll find a way."

"I know, but if he commits any crimes down here and gets arrested, how will we get back at all?"

"Don't worry about that. I promise that we'll get back just fine."

"Okay. I'm sure I'm just worrying about nothing. I know I can trust Lobster."

"It'll all be all right. Come here."

Alex puts his arm around Primavera. He pulls her close. He kisses her neck. Primavera giggles.

"Stop that!" she says

Alex keeps kissing her neck. He pushes her down on to the bed. She giggles. She playfully pushes him.

"No, no. No more."

"No? No?" Alex says in a mocking tone.

He kisses Primavera on the mouth. Primavera moans. She puts her arms around Alex.

•

Larry pulls out of the hotel parking lot. Alex and Primavera are in the backseat. Larry drives out of the town. He turns into a side road.

"The ranch I need to go to is just up this way," Larry says.

He drives down the road. He stops at a gate. He gets out. He buzzes an intercom on the gate.

"¿Qué deseas?" the voice from the intercom says.

"Me llamo Larry. Luis Piedra me habló de ti. Quiero comprar algunas mercancías," Larry says.

"¿Estás solo?"

"No. Tengo tres amigos conmigo. Sólo les estoy dando un paseo."

"Entrar. Usted puede entrar por la puerta principal. Deje a sus amigos en el coche."

A buzz comes from the gate. The gate opens. Larry gets back in the car. He drives up the path. He parks the car. He gets out. He gives the keys to Alex.

"I'll be back in a little bit," Larry says. "If it gets too hot, you can start the car and turn on the AC. Don't run it too long. I want to save on gas."

Larry walks up to the ranch house. He knocks on the door. The door opens. Larry goes inside. A man in a cowboy hat comes out. He stands in front of the door. He watches the car.

"That's a big house," Alex says.

The turntable is on Alex's lap. The Arcesia record is on the turntable.

"What did Lobster say he was doing?" John says.

"He said he was buying merchandise," Primavera says. "I don't like the sound of that."

"He's probably just scoring grass. It's not a big deal. It's just cheaper down here."

"I figured. I hope he actually isn't. I don't want to try to go back across the border with that in the car."

"Lobster does this all the time," Alex says. "You know how he is. He's always got his little schemes and thinks letting people in on them is going to ruin them. You don't have to worry. We'll be just fine."

"I really hope you're right." Primavera says.

Alex and Primavera sit in the car. John sings "Speedy Gonzales" by Pat Boone. He sings "El Paso" by Marty Robbins. Alex reaches over the driver seat. He starts the car. He turns the air conditioner on. Primavera yawns. She takes a book out of Alex's backpack. She starts reading it. Alex reaches in the front. He turns off the car.

"What's taking him so long?" Primavera says.

"I don't know," Alex says.

There is a knock on the window. The man in the cowboy hat is standing outside.

"Where'd he come from?" Alex says.

He points a gun at Alex and Primavera. Alex and Primavera recoil. Alex knocks the turntable on the floor.

"¡Salgan! ¡Ahora!" the man in the cowboy hat says.

He motions for them to come out.

Alex and Primavera get out of the car. They keep their hands raised. The man in the cowboy hat points to the ranch house.

"¡Movimiento! ¡Ándale!"

Alex and Primavera walk toward the ranch house. The man in the cowboy hat follows. He keeps his gun raised.

*Track 4*


Larry, Alex, and Primavera are in a large basement. There are red stains on the concrete floor.

"I hope that's not what I think it is," Larry says.

"Lobster, what the hell happened?" Alex says. "Why did they take our phones and throw us in here?"

"The guy I tried to buy my shit from is nuts. I got a bad feeling from him when he sat across from me. He insisted on drinking and bullshitting with me. He brought up someone I knew from Alamo Azul that disappeared with the town. Then he suddenly got really fucking upset. He pulled a gun and screamed at me to tell him what I knew. I nearly shit my pants and told him I didn't know anything.

I don't know what I said or did, but he's convinced I'm behind it or something."

"Who the hell did you know from that town?"

"Just the guy I bought my shit from."

"Alex, I'm really scared. What are they going to do to us?" Primavera says.

"We'll find a way out," Alex says.

He looks around the basement. He sees a window.

"We can try through that. It's high up, but if we stand on each other's shoulders, we can reach it."

"It's so small though," Primavera says.

"I think it'll be just big enough for you to squeeze through."

"Me? What am I supposed to do?"

"You can go get help. Go back into town and tell the police."

"No!" Larry says. "The last thing we need is fucking police! How is she supposed to get through the gate anyway?"

"The gate isn't very tall," Primavera says. "I can climb it."

"And just walk back?" Larry says.

"We don't have much choice," Alex says. "I don't want the police either, but who else do we go to?"

"Shit, I guess you're right."

The door into the basement opens. Three men walk down the stairs. The man in front wears a bright green suit. He wears a bolo tie with a red steer skull. The two men behind him carry rifles. They stand in front of Larry, Alex, and Primavera.

"You, the cripple, step forward," the man in the bright green suit says.

Larry raises his hands.

"Look, Pablo, I told you everything I know already. I don't..."

One of the men with a rifle grabs Larry by the collar. He throws Larry to the floor. Pablo steps on Larry's claw hand. Larry yelps.

"I don't think you're being honest," Pablo says.

"I only bought drugs from Jorge! I never even met his sister! I swear!"

"Isabella said it was an American."

Pablo digs his heel into Larry's claw hand.

"Fuck!" Larry says. "Am I the only American she ever met? Did she talk about my hand? I'd think she'd remember that."

"Where are Jorge and Isabella now?"

"I'm telling you, I don't know! Ow!"

Pablo takes his foot off Larry's claw hand.

"Let me show you something," Pablo says.

He reaches in his jacket. He pulls out a magazine. He throws it on the floor. The title of the magazine is *¡Alarma!*. It shows a corpse with its head bashed it. Its clothes are soaked with blood. One of its eyeballs hangs out.

Primavera gasps. She slaps her hand over her mouth. Alex hugs her. They back away.

"Do you see that?" Pablo says. "That's the last bastard who tried to fuck with me. You take a look through that magazine. It describes exactly what happened to him. I'll do worse to all three of you if I find out you're lying."

Pablo walks up the stairs. He is followed by the two men with rifles.

"You have until tomorrow. If you feel like confessing before then, I'll spare your two friends," he says.

He shuts the door.

Larry stands up. He rubs his claw hand. He groans.

"Lobster, what the fuck is going on?" Alex says.

Larry shakes his head.

"Okay, okay. So, I knew this guy's son. He lived in Alamo Azul. Pablo's daughter lived there, too. When he went and visited, he found out she was pregnant. He got pissed and made her tell him who did it. Apparently, she said she was too drunk to remember his name or what he looked like. She just remembered he was an American. Jorge mentioned me to Pablo before and I'm the only guy from America he knew associated with any of his family. That's why he thinks I did it. He's fucking crazy."

"Did you have sex with her?" Primavera says.

"No! I was telling the truth. I never even met her. Now those two are gone with the town. He thinks I was involved with that, too."

"Why is that?"

"He probably thinks I was trying to cover up knocking up his daughter. Getting rid of her and any possible witnesses. I don't know how he thinks I did it."

"Jesus fuck," Alex says. "We have to get out of here. Come on."

Larry, Alex, and Primavera walk to a spot under the window. Alex climbs on Larry's shoulders. Primavera climbs up Larry. She climbs up Alex. She stands on Alex's shoulders. She pushes the window open. She climbs through the window. Her hips get stuck.

"I can't move!" Primavera says.

"Lift me up a little, Lobster," Alex says.

Larry stands on his toes. He pushes Alex up by his feet. Alex grabs Primavera's ass. He pushes her. She doesn't move. He pushes harder.

"Hurry up!" Larry says. "I can't hold you much longer."

Alex pulls his hands back. He shoves Primavera by her ass. She slides through the window.

"Ouch!"

Primavera stands up. She brushes her skirt off. She rubs her ass. Larry collapses. Alex falls on top of him.

Primavera kneels. She looks through the window.

"Are you guys okay?"

Alex climbs off Larry.

"Yeah, we're okay," Alex says. "Hurry up and get out before someone sees you."

"I'll be back soon. I promise."

Primavera runs away.

Larry stands up. He adjusts his collar. He brushes his pants.

"You need to stop dating chicks with fat asses," he says.

"Larry, shut the hell up. I am not in the mood," Alex says.

"All right, all right. Sorry. Fuck."

Alex picks up the magazine on the floor. He looks at the cover.

"Did that guy really do this?" he says.

"Pablo? I don't know. I've only heard about him from Jorge. He did say his dad could be brutal to his enemies."

"So why the fuck were you trying to buy drugs from him?"

"I didn't know it was him. I just asked around where the best place to buy shit was and they pointed me to this ranch."

Alex holds up the magazine.

"If Pri doesn't get help on time, we're going to end up like this. Did you really have to stop here?"

"It was your idea to come down here in the first place."

Alex tosses the magazine to the floor.

"Yes, and if it was up to me, we would have gone straight to Mexico City."

"Pardon the fuck out of me for trying to make some money off this trip like you're trying to. Do you know how cheap I usually get weed and pills here? I would have made a big profit back home if everything went right. You didn't even know if we would find that singer or not."

Alex sits on the floor.

"Fuck it," he says. "Arguing isn't going to solve anything."

Larry lies on the floor. He clutches his claw hand.

"Christ, my fucking hand hurts. That guy was heavy as shit."

"Ah, shit!" Alex says.

"What?"

"I should have told Pri to grab John."

"He's still in the car?"

"Yeah. I hope he's all right."

"Well, shit. Another thing to worry about. Hurry back, Pri!"

•

Alex sits with his back against the wall. He looks out of the window. It is night outside. The moon is full. The basement is almost pitch black.

"Hey, you still awake, Lobster?"

"Yeah. It's kind of hard to sleep under these circumstances."

"I hope Pri is okay."

"If she's not, we're all screwed."

"I shouldn't have made her go. I'm so worried about her."

"She can take care of herself. Besides, you were right. Neither of us would have been able to fit through the window."

"I hope she gets back soon."

There is a flash of bright light. Larry covers his face. Alex shields his eyes. He looks at the light. There is a glowing face. The face looks around. It disappears.

"What the shit was that?" Larry says.

"It looked like a glowing face."

"What the fuck? Who did it look like?"

Alex shrugs.

"It was too bright to really tell. I just saw a face."

"I swear to Christ, if I survive this, I'm never coming back to this goddamn country."

•

Alex and Larry lay asleep on the floor. The door to the basement swings open. Alex and Larry wake up. Pablo walks down the stairs. He carries a chainsaw. Three men follow him. Two of them carry rifles. One carries a charcoal grill. One of the men points his gun at Alex. He makes him back up against the wall. The other man with a gun forces Larry to the ground. He stands on Larry's back. Larry grunts. The man with the grill opens it. He sprays lighter fluid on the coals. He lights it. Pablo steps on Larry's arm. Pablo looks around.

"Where is the girl?" Pablo says.

"She's gone," Alex says.

"No matter. My men will find her later. Maybe I'll spare her and let her work in one of my brothels."

Alex clenches his fists.

"I know you're a liar. Even if I can't prove it. You're certainly the one who violated my little girl and then took both my children away," Pablo says. "Here is what I'm going to do. I'm going to cut that lobster claw off you. I'm going to cook it on that grill. Your friend over there is going to eat it."

"Fuck you I will!" Alex says.

The guard hits his stomach with the butt of his rifle. Alex doubles over. He clutches his stomach.

"I'll make sure you eat it, gringo," Pablo says. "That will be day one. It will continue until your cripple friend tells me where Jorge and Isabella are."

"Jesus Christ! I don't know! I don't fucking know!" Larry says.

Pablo starts the chainsaw. He begins to lower it to Larry's claw hand.

There is a gunshot. The head of the man guarding Alex bursts open. He falls to the ground. Blood and brain meat are scattered around him. Everyone turns to the stairs. A man in a balaclava and a cowboy hat stands at the top. He is wearing fatigues. He holds a rifle.

He turns to the man standing on Larry's back. He shoots the man in the gut. The man falls off Larry. Larry jerks his arm. He rolls away. Pablo trips. He drops the chainsaw. He falls forward. He scrapes his face on the running blade. He screams. He writhes on the floor. He clutches his face. Blood pours out of his cheek.

The man by the grill pulls a pistol out of his pants. He shoots at the man on the stairs. He misses. The man on the stairs shoots him in the shoulder. The man on the stairs shoots him in the chest. He falls to the ground.

Larry stands up. He runs up to Pablo. He kicks Pablo in the face. Pablo screams.

"¡Hijo de puta! ¡Te mataré!" he says.

"¡Ustedes dos!" The man on the stairs says. "¡Síganme! ¡Ándale!"

"Alex, he wants us to follow him!" Larry says. "Let's go!"

Larry and Alex run to the stairs. Larry stops. He grabs the grill. He pours the burning coals on Pablo. Pablo screams. He rolls across the floor. He crawls away. He collapses.

Alex is at the stairs.

"Lobster! Come on!"

Larry tosses the grill aside. He runs to Alex. Larry and Alex run up the stairs. They follow the man in the balaclava through the ranch house. Two other men try to block the front door. They pull out pistols. The man in the balaclava shoots them both. They collapse on the ground. He leads Larry and Alex outside. He leads them to Larry's car. A pickup truck is parked next to it. A man in a balaclava and an army cap sits behind the wheel.

"¡Entra en tu coche y síguenos!" The man in the balaclava and cowboy hat says. "¡No pares para nada!"

Gunshots come from the ranch house. Several men run out. Larry gets behind the wheel of his car. Alex dives in the backseat. The pickup truck peels away. Larry follows close behind. Alex tumbles in the backseat. They follow the truck to the gate. The gate has been blown open. They drive out of the ranch. A jeep follows them. Men shoot at them from the jeep. The pickup truck speeds up. Larry speeds up. The truck leads them down several turns. The jeep falls behind.

The pickup truck slows down. Larry slows his car down.

*Track 5*

Larry grips the wheel of the car hard. He breathes heavily.

"Holy fuck. Holy fucking shit. What the fuck?"

Alex picks up the portable turntable from the floor. He reaches under the seat. He pulls out the Arcesia record. He puts the record on the turntable.

"John, are you okay?" Alex says.

"Alex! There you are, man. What happened?" John says.

"I'm still trying to process that myself."

"Are YOU okay, man?"

"At some point I will be."

"Where are we now?"

"Good question. Lobster, where are we?"

"I'd like to know that too," Larry says. "No idea where these two are taking us."

"We're following someone? Who are they?" John says.

"I don't know that either. If I had to guess, I'd say it's a rival cartel," Alex says.

"I fucking hope not," Larry says. "I've had enough of those kinds of assholes. I'm fucking done with the Mexican fucking mafia. I don't care how cheap they sell anymore."

"I just hope they know where Pri is," Alex says.

"What happened to her?" John says.

"I sent her to get help. I don't know where she is. I'm so fucking stupid. I should have never sent her. If she's hurt, I'll never forgive myself."

"Don't worry, bro," Larry says. "I'm sure she's okay. These guys will probably lead us right to her."

"I really hope so," Alex says.

•

The pickup truck leads Larry and Alex to a small village. Many of the buildings look abandoned. There are words painted on them.

"¡Ya basta!"

"¡Para todos todo!"

"¡No pasarán!"

"¡Todas las cosas no son nada para mi!"

"Contra la policía. Contra los carteles."

"What do all those say?" Alex says.

"It's a bunch of political slogans," Larry says. "These guys must be terrorists or something,"

"Well, if they are, they still saved us. We don't have much choice but to trust them."

The pickup truck stops in front of a house. There is a portrait of a woman with a red bandanna on her face painted on the house. Larry pulls up beside the pickup truck. The two men get out of the pickup truck. Larry and Alex get out of their car.

Alex walks up to the two men. He shakes their hands.

"Thank you so much. Um. Gracias. Um. Me llamo Alex."

"Do you speak English?" The man in the army cap says.

"Yeah, I do. Sorry. My Spanish is terrible."

"It's all right. My name is Diego. This is my brother, Alonso."

He points to the man in the cowboy hat.

"Unfortunately, he speaks no English."

Larry walks up to the Diego, Alonso, and Alex.

"Muchas gracias, chicos," Larry says. "Casi me he despedazado por ese psicópata."

"De nada," Alonso says.

"Hey, have you guys seen a girl around? She's about shoulder height to me, long black hair. She had on a blue blouse and a black skirt." Alex says.

"Primavera?" Diego says.

"Yes! You know her?"

"We found her on the side of the road last night. She flagged us down and we picked her up. We brought her back here. She was the one who told us where you were."

"See, Alex?" Larry says. "I told you she'd be okay."

"Where is she?" Alex says.

"She's in there," Diego says.

He points to the house with the portrait painted on it.

Alex runs to the house. He goes inside. Primavera is sitting at a table. A woman is across from her. She has long silver hair. It is tied in a ponytail. She looks around her late 60's. The woman has a rifle sitting next to her.

"Pri!" Alex says.

Primavera turns to Alex. She gets up. She runs to him. They embrace. They kiss.

"Thank God you're okay," Alex says. "I'm sorry I let you go alone."

"Don't worry about that, bebé," Primavera says. "I'm just relieved they got you out."

Alex sees Primavera is wearing fatigues.

"Did they recruit you?"

Primavera laughs.

"Nah. My clothes were dirty and this is all they had."

"I told you my boys would bring your novio back," the older woman says.

Larry, Diego, and Alonso walk in to the house. Diego and Alonso take off their hats. They take off their balaclavas.

"Hey Pri, glad to see you're doing okay," Larry says.

"You too. No more trying to buy drugs down here, okay?" Primavera says.

"Yeah, no. That's not happening again. Sorry I almost got us all killed."

"If we die down here, I'll never forgive you."

"You'll all be safe with us," the older woman says. "You all must be very hungry. Diego, Alonso, ayúdame a hacer la cena."

•

Larry, Alex, and Primavera sit at the table with Diego, Alonso, and the woman. They eat tamales. The portable turntable is on the floor. The Arcesia record spins on the turntable. The woman introduces herself as Sofía. She says Diego and Alonso are her sons. She asks Alex why he and his friends came to Mexico. Alex tells her about Y. Bhekhirst. He tells her about the letter. He tells her about the border guards. He tells her what happened at Pablo's ranch.

"I see," Sofía says. "Will you continue to Mexico City to find the singer?"

"We may as well," Alex says. "We need to let things cool off before we try to get back to the States."

"You must be very careful. Pablo's men will certainly be looking for you."

"Believe me, we know," Larry says. "We're heading straight to Mexico City and straight back. No more detours."

"They are awful men," Sofia says. "Never have dealings with the cartels. I lost my beloved husband to those creatures."

"I'm so sorry," Primavera says.

Sofía looks at her plate.

"I remember when I first met him. The McOndo Corporation wanted to build a luxury resort over my little hometown. The federal government was forcing us to sell our homes. Most of us refused. They wanted to send in the Federales to evict us. But then a group of men and women came to protect us. La Unión they called themselves. They helped us keep the Federales at bay. The man who would be my husband was among them. Manuel. He was a beautiful man with a fierce hatred of injustice.

"The Federales tried sending a negotiator, but Manuel sent him away with the same message each time he came. Leave us be. They could have brought the whole weight of the government down on us, but the McOndo Corporation backed out. They knew the bad international press from the Federales raiding us would severely damage the reputation of the resort. So they gave up.

"That wasn't the end of it. After they left, it began to snow, even though it was the middle of summer. It didn't stop. The cold and snow were so oppressive, we all had to abandon the town. Now it's an uninhabitable arctic nightmare."

"That's awful!" Primavera says. "Any idea what caused that?"

"I suspect the Federales negotiator. I believe he called himself Señor Humo. I always got a bad feeling from him. Like something evil was living inside him. I joined La Unión after that. I married my beautiful Manuel and we had these two wonderful sons who you sit next to.

"About 30 years ago, we attempted to organize several factory workers into a more radical union. What we didn't know is the union they were already a part of had its leadership intertwined with a cartel. Those beasts captured five of our men, including my husband, and beheaded them all. They sent us the heads with insults written on their foreheads. We were forced to give up. The factory workers wanted nothing to do with us after that. However, we still managed to track down the men responsible. We took our revenge on them. We gave them more dignified deaths than men like that deserve. But, of course, it didn't bring my husband nor my comrades back.

"Since then, we've put our efforts into protecting the innocent from the cartels, as well as the state and the capitalists. After all, what real difference is there between them? The cartels are monsters, but at least they lay their brutality bare for all to see."

"I dig. It's hard to argue that," John says from the turntable.

"It must be lonely in that record," Sofía says.

"You don't know the half of it. I'm hoping that I can find someone down here who could maybe get me out."

"I see. We have someone who may be able to help."

"No kidding?"

"Yes. I'll take you to them when we finish eating."

"Thank you so much for everything," Alex says. "I don't know how we'll ever repay you."

"Perhaps you can," Sofía says. "We have a couple members who are musicians. They want to spread our message through song. If you could speak with them and write about them for an American audience, it would greatly help us."

"Yeah, I can definitely do that."

Larry has finished his tamales.

"I don't suppose I can buy weed from you people, can I?" he says.

Everyone except Alonso stares at Larry. Alonso looks around. He stares at Larry.

"I'm kidding! Jesus. Lighten up."

•

Sofía leads Alex to a shack. Alex carries the portable turntable.

"This is where our comrade Cara stays. They assisted you in escaping Pablo. They may be able to help your friend in the record," Sofía says.

"How so?" Alex says. "I only saw Diego and Alonso there."

"They are able to see places from afar. They found where you were being held inside Pablo's hacienda."

"That glowing face I saw."

"Precisely. I don't know the extent of their abilities. They were in this abandoned village when we arrived here. They don't speak, but they have always aided us when we ask for it. Cara is the name they answer most to."

"I hope this cat can help," John says.

Sofía and Alex enter the shack. A woman sits in the middle of the room. She wears no clothes. Her body has patches of what looks like gangrene. She wears a mask with a painting of the Virgin Mary. There are no holes for eyes or a mouth on the mask. She raises her head.

"Cara, este hombre tiene un objeto en el que un fantasma está atrapado dentro," Sofía says. "¿Puede ayudar a sacarlo?"

Cara gestures to the turntable. She gestures to the ground. Alex places the turntable on the ground. Cara waves Sofía and Alex away.

"They want us leave them," Sofía says.

Alex follows Sofía out. He turns to the turntable.

"Good luck, John."

"Hey, Alex?" John says. "If this works and I don't see you again, thanks for everything, man."

"I didn't even think about that. If you do disappear, then thank you too. I hope you know I always liked your music."

Sofía and Alex leave the shack.

•

The sun has gone down. Larry, Alex, and Primavera sit around a fire outside. Alex's laptop is on his lap. There are two men with guitars across from them. They introduce themselves as "La Orquesta de la Huelga General." They play songs for Larry, Alex, and Primavera. They show Alex their lyric notebooks. Larry and Primavera translate them for Alex. Alex asks them questions through Larry and Primavera. Alex types on his laptop. Alex thanks them for their time. They get up and leave.

"Well, even if we don't find Y. Bhekhirst, I've got that interview," Alex says.

"Yeah, I'm sure there's a big market for Mexican anarchist music in America," Larry says.

"I could probably sell it to *Torsion* magazine. They've done articles about Mexican cartels. Plus, there are probably some left-wing publications that would like it."

"You should write a book about this trip," Primavera says. "You can call it *The Search for Y. Bhekhirst*. After what's happened to us, it would be really interesting."

"I don't know. I'm no good at telling stories," Alex says. "Plus, I know if my family read it, they would freak out about what happened. Yours would too, Pri."

"Yeah, and I don't need the world knowing I've been sneaking weed and shit into the States from here," Larry says.

"Believe me, I'm leaving all of that out in my articles."

Larry, Alex, and Primavera look into the fire.

"Do you really think John might disappear?" Primavera says.

"It's possible," Alex says. "That Cara woman apparently can't talk so she didn't say anything. Sofía said she'd call for me when she was ready."

"I hope if she does get him out, we can at least say goodbye."

Primavera leans against Alex. Alex puts his arm around her.

"I'd hate to see that weird old hippy go," Larry says. "I never liked his singing, but he's a pretty cool guy. For a ghost, I mean."

"I know, but I'm sure he'd be happy to rest," Alex says. "Living inside that record can't be fun."

"Let's get back to that room Sofía prepared for us," Larry says. "It's getting cold out here."

*Track 6*

Alex wakes up to a bright light. He opens his eyes. There is a glowing face floating above him. Alex jumps out of the bed.

"Fuck!" he says.

The face disappears. Larry and Primavera wake up. They sit up in their beds.

"What's wrong, Alex?" Primavera says.

"Uh, I think Cara wants me to come to her shack," Alex says.

Alex leads Larry and Primavera to Cara's shack. They enter. A man sits in the middle of the room. There are tribal markings on his body. He wears a mask with

Nahuatl writing on it. There are no holes for eyes or mouth on the mask. The portable turntable sits in front of him. The needle is off the Arcesia record.

"I thought you said he was a she," Larry whispers to Alex.

"They were when I came yesterday," Alex whispers to Larry.

"Hola, Cara," Primavera says. "¿Fué capaz de ayudar a nuestro amigo en el disco de vinilo?"

Cara nods.

"Ask her, um, him where John is," Alex says.

Cara holds up a finger.

"Oh, do you understand English?"

Cara nods. He reaches for the turntable needle. He places the needle on the record's label. The record spins. The upper half of a man appears above the turntable. He is transparent. He wears a Hawaiian shirt. The pattern is maps of Hawaii. He has salt-and-pepper hair and beard. He looks to be in his mid-60's.

"John? Is that you?" Alex says.

The man nods.

"Yep, it's me. Looks like this cat couldn't get me out. Not all the way at least."

Cara shrugs.

"At least I can see better," John says. "Used to be I could only see flashes of what was around."

"Yeah, and I can see your face now," Larry says. "It always felt like I was talking to you on a phone or some shit."

"Sorry, John," Primavera says. "We'll find someone who'll get you all the way out."

Alex picks up the turntable.

"Thanks anyway, Cara," he says.

Cara nods.

Alex carries the turntable out of the shack. Larry and Primavera follow him.

"What did he do?" Alex says.

"I don't even know, man," John says. "You left me there and then there was just nothing. Not even the flashes I usually saw. Then, all of a sudden, it was like I dropped acid again after all these years. Just colors everywhere. Colors that I saw, colors that I tasted, colors that I heard. Everything started spinning. It was trippy as hell, man. Then it was like someone stepped on the brakes. I looked around and I could see things clearly. That Cara cat was sitting there in the dark. He shook his head and I guess he took the needle off the record. Then it was like I fell asleep until you guys came."

"Sounds like it sucked," Larry says.

"Nah, man. It was pretty cool. I'm still stuck here, but I feel far out."

Larry, Alex, Primavera, and John arrive back at Sofía's house. Sofía greets them at the front door.

"My friends, I hate to do this, but I must ask you to go to the cellar," Sofia says.

"What's going on?" Alex says.

"Our watchmen have spotted a couple of jeeps heading towards our village. We expect the worst."

"Oh, fuck," Larry's says. "Pablo's guys?"

"Not from what our watchmen have reported. However, we still have reason to believe it's another cartel. What's worse, Cara is supposed to be using their abilities to divert outsiders. Someone who can see past their illusion is coming. Please, go to the cellar for your safety. Diego will lead you."

Larry, Alex, Primavera, and John enter the house. Diego wears his balaclava. He holds a rifle. He leads them to the cellar.

"I'll come back and get you when this is over," Diego says. "Try to keep quiet. That window has no glass. They'll hear you outside."

He closes the cellar door.

"Well, this is familiar," Larry says.

"We'll be okay," Primavera says. "I know we're safe with these people protecting us."

"I hope you're right."

The sound of cars pulling up comes through the window. Doors open and close. There are footsteps. There are guns being cocked.

"Come on," Alex whispers. "Let's go hear what's happening."

Larry, Alex, Primavera, and John gather by the window. They press against the wall.

"¿Quién eres y por qué estás aquí?" they hear Sofía say.

"You speak English? Eh. Ob-lay een-glesh? I'm not so good with the Spanish," a man says.

"I said, 'Who are you and why have you come here?'"

"Relax. I come in peace. I heard through the grapevine that someone here took care of Pablo. He's been a thorn in my side for a while now. I wanted to reward them."

"We know nothing about that."

"Come on, don't lie to me, honey. I could see past that Aztec broo-hereya and I can see past your bullshit."

"We want nothing you have to offer."

"You sure about that? You know, I'm big fan of what you guys are doing. We both hate la poh-lees-eya after all."

"Don't act like a villain from a bad American movie."

A gun cocks.

"You will leave now," Sofía says.

"All right, all right! Crazy fucking broad. I was going to help you dumb-ass terrorists. I guess you don't need it though. I hope you like this shanty town while you have it. You won't be getting anything beyond it. Ever."

There are sounds of hurried footsteps. Car doors slam. Cars speed away.

•

Larry, Alex, Primavera, and John sit at the table with Diego, Alonso, and Sofía. They drink coffee. They eat scrambled eggs.

"Who were the people that came by earlier?" Alex says.

"They were certainly cartel members," Sofía says. "They were led by a man from America. I've never seen that before."

"We overheard you talking to him," Larry says. "Seems like he had something against Pablo."

"It seemed so."

Larry explains what Pablo had told him about his daughter.

"Maybe he's the one who knocked up Pablo's daughter and made that whole town disappear," Larry says.

"It's possible," Sofia says. "He was able to see past Cara's illusions. He may be able to cause that sort of damage. If that is true, then we may be in great danger."

"¿Sientes olor a humo?" Alonso says.

Sofía winces. She smells the air. She gets up. She goes to the kitchen.

"¡Alonso! ¡Diego! ¡Vayan a buscar un cubo de agua!" she says.

Diego and Alonso get up. They run outside. They come back with a bucket of water. They carry it to the kitchen. Larry, Alex, and Primavera follow. There is a fire on the kitchen floor. Diego and Alonso pour the water on it. The fire goes out.

Sofía kneels. She checks the burned floor. She checks around the walls. She looks up at the ceiling.

"What happened?" Alex says.

Sofía stands up.

"Please wait here," she says. "I want to check on our comrades."

Sofía leaves the house.

"One fucking thing after another, isn't it?" Larry says.

•

Everyone in the village is gathered in the village square. Sofía stands on a makeshift stage. She speaks through a bullhorn. Larry, Alex, Primavera, and John stand in the back. Primavera translates to Alex and John.

"She's saying that there's someone dangerous who has their sights on the village. She says she doesn't know if all those small fires from earlier were just a warning or if Cara kept a larger fire from breaking out. She's saying we need to be prepared for the worst."

Sofía gets off the stage. Several other La Unión members strike the stage. Sofía approaches Larry, Alex, Primavera, and John.

"Friends," Sofía says. "I'm afraid it's time for you to be heading off. We can't put you in danger. I got the same feeling from that American that I did from Señor Humo. We're certainly at great risk for something terrible."

"You've done so much for us," Primavera says. "Isn't there anything we can do to help?"

"What the hell can we do?" Larry says. "Just take up guns and help her fight this psycho?"

"Your friend with the claw hand is right." Sofía says. "We've prepared ourselves for occasions like this. It would only put more of a burden on us to protect you. It's best you continue on your journey. Your writer novio spreading our message would be the best thing you all could do to help us."

"I wish I could do a little more," Alex says. "I hope people back in the States will read the article."

"It's appreciated. I hope that some will take our message to heart," Sofía says.

"Hey, how do we get to Mexico City from here?" Larry says. "I don't even know where we are."

"Do you have a map? Bring it to me and I'll show you the way to go," Sofia says.

*Track 7*

Larry turns the car around a bend. He drives up the road. He looks in the rear-view mirror. The bend is gone. Alex, Primavera, and John are in the backseat. Alex types on his laptop. The portable turntable is on Primavera's lap. John's upper half floats above the turntable. He looks out the window.

"This is kind of awkward. It feels like you're sitting on my lap now," Primavera says.

"Hm? You say something?" John says. "Sorry. It's been a while since I could appreciate nature like this. It reminds me of when my old lady and I moved from New York to California."

"Oh, yeah. It must be like being able to see again after being blind," Primavera says.

"It's all so fucking beautiful, man. I should have come down here while I was alive. There was a lot I should have done."

Alex stops typing.

"Hey, it's all right. If we can't get you out of there, we can always make up for lost time," he says.

"Thanks guys," John says.

"We're closer to Mexico City than I thought," Larry says. "We should be there in like a day. And thank Christ. I'm about done with this country."

•

Larry stops at a gas station. He starts filling up the tank.

"I'm going inside to get a snack," Alex says. "Do you want something, Pri?"

"Yeah, can you get me a Sidral Mundet?"

Alex walks into the gas station. He picks up a Carlos V bar. He picks up a bottle of Sidral Mundet. He approaches the counter. The man behind the counter has the head of a vulture. He reads a magazine. There is a TV behind the counter. A news report is on. Pablo lies in a hospital bed. Half his face is burned. The other half is covered in bloody bandages. Alex stops in his tracks. He drops the Carlos V bar. He drops the bottle of Sidral Mundet. The bottle shatters. The man behind the counter squawks at Alex in Spanish.

"Sorry! Um. ¡Me disculpo! I'll pay you for that," Alex says.

He leans out the door.

"Lobster! Come here!"

Larry stops pumping gas. He comes into the gas station.

"What the hell?" Larry says.

Alex points at the TV behind the counter. The man behind the counter is still squawking. Larry yells back. He looks at the TV. He sees Pablo being interviewed. He stops yelling.

"Shit, I was certain that guy was dead," Larry says.

The man behind the counter is still squawking.

"¡Cierra la puta boca!" Larry says.

The man behind the counter goes quiet.

"He's going to be after us," Alex says.

"Okay, okay. The motherfucker's laid up in the hospital. Plus, this newscast says he's way up north from where we are. As long as we keep a low profile, we should be fine."

"I hope you're right."

Larry walks up to the counter. He throws money at the man with the vulture head.

"¡Quédese el cambio, feo!" he says.

The man with the vulture head starts squawking in Spanish again. Alex grabs another bottle of Sidral Mundet. He leaves money on the counter.

"¡Me disculpo!" he says.

The man with the vulture head continues to squawk as Alex leaves. He continues as Larry pulls out of the gas station. The squawking fades as Larry drives down the road.

•

The sun goes down. Larry turns on the headlights. Alex has the portable turntable on his lap. John floats above the turntable.

"You were right, Pri," Alex says. "This is awkward."

John yawns.

"Hey, can you take the needle off, man? I'm clanked."

Alex takes the needle off the record's label. John disappears.

"That's going to take some getting used to," Alex says.

"He's got the right idea. I want to find a place for the night," Larry says.

He holds the map out to Alex.

"Here, check the map. See if there are any places nearby we can stop."

Alex takes the map. He turns on the light in the backseat. He looks over the map.

"If I'm looking at this right, there's nothing for miles," Alex says.

"Shit!" Larry says, "I don't want to have to pull over to the side of the road again. Sleeping in the front seat sucks."

"I really don't want to sleep here again, either," Primavera says. "What if that Pablo guy finds us there?"

"I doubt he'll find us out here," Alex says. "But I doubt I could sleep while thinking about that."

"Fuck. I wish I still had my phone," Larry says.

"Hey, there are some lights over there," Primavera says.

Larry looks out the window.

"Yeah, it might be someone's home," he says. "Maybe we can negotiate a floor for the night or something."

"Are you sure that's a good idea?" Alex says.

"It's either that, or the car again."

•

Larry pulls into the driveway. He stops by a sign. It reads MISIÓN DE SANTA MARIA GORETTI.

"We're in luck. It's a mission," Larry says. "I'm sure we can convince the priest to give a place to sleep for the night."

Larry drives closer to the building. It resembles a Spanish colonial mansion.

"It looks pretty old," Primavera says.

"Yeah, but there are lights on," Alex says. "Someone's got to be in there and awake."

Larry parks. He gets out of the car. Alex and Primavera follow. They walk up to the mission door. Larry knocks. No one answers. Larry knocks harder.

"Maybe no one is in?" Primavera says.

Larry grabs the door handle. He pulls on the door. It opens. The foyer is dimly lit.

"Yeah, no. This is how every horror movie starts. Fuck this," Larry says.

"You were the one that wanted to come here, Lobster," Alex says.

"That was then, this is now."

"So you just want to go back and sleep in the car?" Larry grumbles.

"Fine, let's go. We'll probably die here or some shit. Fucking country, no goddamn hotels or anything nearby."

Larry, Alex, and Primavera walk inside the mission. They look around. The floor is white. There are chairs with bright red velvet upholstery against the wall. Lion heads are carved in the wooden arm rests. Lights resembling torches hang on the wall. A spiral staircase is on the other side of the foyer. There are no other doors. Behind the spiral staircase there is a wall. A large crucifix hangs on it.

"This doesn't look much like a church," Primavera says.

"Looks like a mansion that was converted into a mission," Alex says. "The nave must be in another room."

"Hey! Anyone home?" Larry says.

His voice echoes in the foyer. No one answers.

"You've got guests! We need a place to sleep! Jesus would really appreciate it if you helped us out! ¿Hay alguien ahí?"

No one answers still. Larry, Alex, and Primavera stand in the foyer.

"Maybe the place is abandoned?" Primavera says.

"Then why are there lights on?" Larry says.

"Maybe they're upstairs and they can't hear us," Alex says.

"Well, I guess we may as well go check it out," Larry says.

Alex, Larry, and Primavera walk towards the stairs. They get closer to the crucifix. The Jesus is naked. His wounds are deep. He is covered in blood. He has a look of agony on his face.

"Ech, I've never seen a crucifix look that bloody," Primavera says. "It's kind of scary looking."

"It's not too late to turn back now," Larry says.

"Screw it," Alex says. "Let's just check upstairs. If no one's up there, we'll go back to the car."

Alex looks up the stairs. It's too dark to see the top. He takes out his keychain. He turns on the small flashlight on the keychain. The light seems drowned in the darkness. Alex sighs.

Larry, Alex, and Primavera walk up the stairs. After five minutes they have not reached the top.

"How long are these damn stairs?" Larry says.

"It's getting pretty dark," Alex says. "Pri, can you run down to the car and get a flashlight? I've got a bigger one in my backpack."

"Yeah, I'll be right back."

Primavera runs down the stairs.

Larry and Alex sit on the stairs.

"Why are we doing this? This is stupid," Larry says.

"Probably," Alex says. "But now I'm curious. I want to see what's in here. What's the worst that could happen?"

"You're asking me that after everything that's happened?"

"Good point."

Primavera comes back. She carries a flashlight. Alex checks his watch.

"That was fast," he says.

Primavera looks down the stairs.

"Yeah, that didn't take as long as it did last time," she says. "Something funny is going on with the stairs."

Alex takes the flashlight from Primavera. He aims it upwards. He turns it on. The beam hits the ceiling. Alex sees a hole where the staircase goes through.

"There's the next floor," Alex says. "It's just a little bit up."

Larry, Alex, and Primavera continue up the stairs. They emerge onto the second floor. They look around. They are in a dimly lit hallway. There are several doors. Alex looks down the stairs. The hole is pitch black. He shines the flashlight down the hole. It hits the stairs. He cannot see the bottom.

"All right, let's try these doors," Alex says.

"I hope one of these is a bathroom," Larry says. "I've really got to piss."

They try the first door on the left. It is locked. They try the first door on the right. It opens to an empty room with no windows. They open the second door to the left. It opens into a bathroom.

"Oh, hey. I got lucky for once," Larry says. "You guys try a couple more doors. I'll catch up."

Larry closes the door. Alex and Primavera try the door across the hall. It opens into another empty room. Alex and Primavera try the next door to the left. It opens into a room with blue walls. There are several ringneck parrots walking across the floor. Some are green. Some are blue. Some are yellow.

"Look at that!" Primavera says. "They're all so cute!"

Alex and Primavera enter the room. Primavera bends down. Two of the parrots climb on her hand. Both are green. She pets the parrots.

"They look just like my Makoto," she says.

The door slams shut. The parrots begin to screech. They fly around wildly. They shit on the floor. They shit on Alex and Primavera's shirts. Alex claps his hands over his ears.

"Okay, we need to get out of here," Alex says.

Alex and Primavera run for the door. Alex throws it open. They step back into the hallway. Alex slams the door. He looks around.

"Is Lobster still in that bathroom?" Alex says.

Alex and Primavera walk back to the bathroom door. Alex knocks.

"Hey, are you done in there yet?" he says.

There is no answer. Alex knocks again.

"Lobster? Are you in there?"

"Are you sure that's the right door?" Primavera says.

"Yeah. It has to be," Alex says. "We couldn't have gotten turned around that badly."

Alex turns the knob. The door opens. The room is pitch black.

"Lobster? Are you in here?" he says.

Alex feels the wall for a light switch. He steps into the room. There is no floor. Alex falls. He grabs Primavera's arm. Primavera stumbles. She is pulled down with Alex. She cries out.

Alex and Primavera fall into the blackness.

"Alex!" Primavera says. "Alex, wake up!"

Alex sits up. He rubs his head. He rubs his eyes. He looks around. He is sitting in a field. He is on a red picnic blanket. The grass is bright green. The sky is clear. A forest is on the horizon. Primavera sits next to him.

"Where are we?" Alex says.

"I don't know," Primavera says. "The last thing I remember is that we were falling and I blacked out. When I woke up, we were here."

Alex looks around.

"Are we even still in Mexico?" he says.

"I don't know. It's really nice here though," Primavera says.

"Yeah. It's really peaceful."

A gentle breeze starts blowing. Alex puts his arm around Primavera. He pulls her close. She puts her head on his shoulder. They watch the grass sway.

The wind picks up. Alex turns Primavera towards him. He kisses her deeply. She moans. He pushes her on her back. He kisses her hungrily. The wind blows harder. Clouds roll in quickly. The blue sky becomes gray.

Alex pulls Primavera's skirt up. Thunder booms in the sky. He tears her panties off. Rain pours down. The wind blows harder and faster. He unzips his pants. He pulls his hard cock out. He kisses her lips and neck. He thrusts himself into her. She moans. She wraps her arms around him. Lightning strikes nearby. Thunder rolls. The rain pours down harder. He kisses her mouth. He thrusts into her faster. The thunder cracks even louder than before. Lightning strikes again. He cums inside her. Primavera throws her head back. Her body trembles. She cries out.

Alex and Primavera hold each other. The wind dies down. The rain tapers off. The clouds part. They lay on the picnic blanket. Their clothes are soaked. They fall asleep. The sky clears. The sun shines down.

·

Alex wakes up. Primavera is next to him. His clothes are still damp. He sits up. He wakes up Primavera.

"Hey, you all right?" Alex says.

"Yeah, I feel great."

She kisses Alex.

"That was amazing," she says.

"It was. You just seemed so beautiful right then. When that storm came, I thought the sky was going to crack in half, but I didn't care. Not even a tornado could have blown us apart."

Primavera hugs Alex. He holds her close.

"How long were we asleep for?" Alex says.

"No idea," Primavera says.

"We'd better go. We still need to find Lobster," Alex stands up.

He looks around. He sees a barn nearby.

"Let's try over there."

Alex and Primavera walk to the barn. They open the door. The barn is empty. There is a door in the loft. They climb the ladder to the loft. Alex opens the door. It leads back into the hallway in the mission. They enter the hall. Alex looks down the hall. They came from the first door on the left from the staircase.

"Lobster!" Alex says. "Lobster! Where are you at?"

"Hey!" Larry's voice comes from the staircase hole. "Hey, I'm downstairs!"

Alex and Primavera run down the stairs. Larry is in the foyer.

"Where have you guys been?" Larry says.

"We were trying to find you," Alex says. "What happened to you?"

"Screw it, I'll explain it in the car. It's morning so we should get going."

"Morning?" Primavera says. "How long have we been in here? What day is it?"

"I don't know," Larry says. "Christ, I wish I still had my phone. I'm buying a prepaid one when we get to Mexico City."

Alex looks at his watch.

"Looks like it's 6:30 A.M.," he says. "Hopefully we were only here for a night. We've already lost too much time."

•

Larry pulls the car back onto the road. Alex and Primavera sit in the backseat. Alex brings the portable turntable to his lap. He puts the needle on the Arcesia record label. John appears. He yawns.

"Hey, man," John says. "Anything happen while I was sleeping?"

Alex explains what happened in the mission. He tells about the stairs. He tells about the doors. He tells about the fields. He tells about the storm. He leaves out the part about making love to Primavera.

"Crazy shit," John says.

"So, what happened to you, Lobster?" Primavera says.

Larry sighs.

"Okay, so after I got done taking a piss, I went back in the hall, but it was different. All the doors were gone, except one at the other end of the hall. Even the hole to the staircase was gone. Just an empty floor like it was never there. I decided to try that other door. I went through it and it went out onto this beach. It was the middle of the night. The beach looked real nice so I figured I'd check it out. When I stepped out, the door slammed shut. That's when I noticed it wasn't attached to anything. It sat there in the middle of the fucking sand leading to nothing. I tried opening it, but it tipped over. It was just a goddamn detached door. The beach was at the bottom of some big ass cliff, so there was nowhere to go but along the beach. It seemed to go on forever in either direction. I picked up the door and threw it. I was fucking pissed, figuring I was trapped.

"I started walking along the beach until I calmed down. I looked out at the water. The way the moon reflected on the water looked real pretty. I stopped being angry about being trapped and thought for a little bit. I tested the water with my hand. It was a lot warmer than I expected. Since there was nowhere else to go, I thought maybe if I swam out, I'd find something. I stripped down to my boxers and left my clothes on the beach.

"I dove in the water and swam for a while. I found an entrance to an underwater cave. I went up for air and dove back in, hoping it would get me somewhere. It turned out not to be such a great idea. The tunnel was longer than I could hold my breath for. I'd gone too far in. There was no way I could have swam out and gone up for air before I drowned. I swam faster, praying to fucking God there was somewhere I could go up. I got lucky. I came to an opening and swam up as fast as I could. Once I caught my breath, I realized I was in a cavern. I got out of the water and saw there was a hole in the ceiling of the cavern. It looked like the moon was directly above. Under the hole, there were blankets. I was so fucking tired, I took my boxers off to dry and climbed under the blankets to sleep. It was strangely warm and comfortable in there.

"When I woke up, it was still night. My clothes were next to me, folded neatly, and so was that door. I had no idea who brought them or how they got them there, but the door stood like it was actually attached to hinges this time, even though it wasn't. I opened it and it led back into the hallway. The hallway looked like it was back to normal. Thank fucking Christ. I got dressed and went in.

"I called out for you guys and tried the doors, but they were all locked. I went back downstairs and you weren't there either. I was still tired so I went to sleep in one of those chairs. When I woke up again, I checked outside. It looked like it was the crack of dawn. That's when you called out to me."

"It sounds like you had a terrible time," Primavera says.

"I don't know," Larry says. "I wouldn't say that. That beach really was beautiful. The swim sucked but at the same time it was kind of pleasant. The whole experience was almost like being right on the line between being on a nice buzz and being way too fucked up. Except without being hungover afterwards."

"Looks like I missed some far out shit," John says.

"You're lucky," Larry says. "We're going straight to Mexico City. Fuck this shit."

*Track 9*

Larry parks his car in the Holiday Inn parking lot. He gets out of the car. He scratches his head with his claw hand.

"God, that traffic was awful," he says. "Thank Christ we're finally here."

Alex and Primavera get out of the backseat. Alex carries John on the portable turntable.

"So, what's the plan from here?" John says.

"After we check in, I'm going to see if I can find Pepe Díaz in the phone book," Alex says. "I couldn't find a number online, but maybe he'll be there. If not, we'll just drop by."

"Alex, I swear to God," Larry says. "If we came here for nothing, I'm killing your ass."

"You won't do that. You'd miss me."

"I'd sell you to Pablo for a fucking Cubano sandwich."

•

Larry, Alex, Primavera, and John are in Larry's hotel room. Primavera sits on the bed. John on the portable turntable is next her. Larry sits in the chair at the desk. Alex looks through the phone book.

"There are a lot of Pepe Díazes, but here's one whose address matches the envelope," Alex says.

He picks up the phone. He dials the number. The phone rings.

"¿Bueno?" a man's voice says.

"Hello," Alex says. "Uh, do you speak English?"

"I do. Who is this?" The man speaks with no accent.

"My name's Alex. I'm a music writer. Do you know Y. Bhekhirst?"

"Oh, dear. It's been a while since I heard that name. You actually listened to that album?"

"Yeah, I'm a huge fan of it. I'd like to interview you."

The man laughs.

"Are you serious?" he says.

"Uh, yeah. Is that okay?"

The man laughs again.

"Well, if you really want to. Come by around four. I'll make dinner and we can talk over it."

"Oh, that's too kind. You don't have to do that."

"Oh no, it's not a big deal. I don't take many guests anymore. I used to be a journalist too. I've always believed in helping the next generation."

"Do you mind if I bring a few friends then?"

"Yes, that's no problem at all. How many?"

"Three."

"Sure! Just let me know if you want to invite any more. All of you are welcome! You know where I am?"

"Yeah, I got your address from the phone book."

"Great, so four o'clock. I'll see you then, friend!"

Alex hangs up the phone.

"Well?" Larry says.

"Great news," Alex says. "I've got the interview and I got us a free dinner."

"I knew I was friends with you for a reason," Larry says.

"That's great!" Primavera says.

"I'm interested in meeting this cat," John says. "He must be an interesting guy to make the tunes he did."

"Oh, yeah," Alex says. "I didn't tell him you were a ghost. I hope he doesn't mind."

•

Larry pulls up to the house. It is on the outskirts of Mexico City. Larry, Alex, and Primavera get out of the car. Primavera carries the turntable and John. Alex carries his laptop bag. He knocks on the door. A man opens it. His hair is white and curly. He has a large mustache. He looks to be in his early 70's. He wears a white dress shirt and black dress pants. He smiles.

"You must be Alex! Welcome to mi casa," the man says. "And these must be the friends you told me about. Come on in and you can introduce me."

Larry, Alex, Primavera, and John enter the house. Primavera sets the turntable on the floor.

"Ah, one of your friends is a ghost," the man says. "I don't see many folks around here being friendly with ghosts. I don't know why. Most of them are lovely people."

"Hey, man," John says. "Name's John."

"Pepe is the name I go by these days," the man says. "Are you stuck in that record?"

"Yeah. Only way I can talk with people is if they play it with the needle on the label."

"I know someone who might be able to help."

"Really? Cool, man! I met someone else who tried, but couldn't do much."

"This person will certainly be able to help. They're quite amazing. I'll get a hold of them later. Who's this lovely young lady?"

"Hi," Primavera says. "I'm Primavera. Everyone calls me Pri."

She extends her hand. Pepe kisses her hand.

"It's a pleasure to meet you. Is this your lady, Alex?"

Alex nods.

"Such a beautiful creature. Are you from here in Mexico?"

"No, I was born in Spain, but I've lived in America most of my life."

"Spain! A fascinating country. I learned a lot about it in my younger years."

Pepe turns to Larry. He raises his hand. He sees Larry's claw. He raises his other hand. Larry shakes it.

"What's your name, sir?"

"Name's Larry. Friends call me 'Lobster' cause of..."

Larry holds his claw up.

"I see. People used to call me Gringo Viejo when I first came here. The people that called me that are long gone now."

"You originally from the States?"

Pepe nods.

"I first came down here a long time ago. I went back up for a few years back in the 80's. I didn't like how the country had changed, so I came back down."

"Was that when you recorded the album?" Alex says.

"Oh, yes, the album," Pepe says. "Dinner is almost ready. Please, have a seat. We'll discuss it in just a moment."

•

Larry, Alex, Primavera, and John sit around the table. Alex is typing on his laptop. Pepe brings frijoles negros, rice, and Negra Modelo beer. He sets a plate in front of everyone except John.

"Man, I wish I could still eat," John says. "That grub looks so good."

"It seems so rude to eat in front of a guest who can't enjoy the meal," Pepe says.

"Nah, man. It's a drag, but don't let me stop you."

Pepe sits down.

"So, what do you want to know, Mr. Alex?" he says.

"I guess I'll start with the obvious question," Alex says, "What does the name 'Y. Bhekhirst' mean?"

"I don't know."

"You don't know?"

"I didn't pick the name."

"Were you a part of the band?"

"If you can call two fellows a band. I played the drums while the other gentleman did everything else. I didn't even play on all the songs."

"So it wasn't your project."

"It was not. While I was in New York City, I took up drums. After practicing for about a year or so, I answered a newspaper ad of someone who was looking for a drummer. He was a young Latin fellow named José. He played a tape of a couple songs he had done. They weren't very good, but I thought they were just demos. He wasn't a great musician, but he had an infectious enthusiasm.

"We put together a few more songs. We agreed that only one was particularly good, so he had that pressed as a single. I didn't think we had enough for a passable album, but he had one made anyway. He was crediting us both under pseudonyms anyway, so I didn't mind too much. Nobody bought the album and it got no reviews, so I didn't bother doing anything else with the man. We still keep in touch, however."

Larry chugs his beer. He sighs.

"So, basically, you aren't the guy we're looking for," Larry says. "Alex..."

"Calm down, Lobster," Alex says. "So where is the man you worked with at now?"

"He lives in Peru."

"Fucking Peru," Larry says. "Can I have another beer?"

"Certainly," Pepe says.

"You don't happen to have any tequila, do you?"

"Of course! Just a moment."

Pepe gets up from the table.

"Lobster, calm the fuck down," Alex says.

"I'm trying to stay calm," Larry says. "That's why I need more to drink."

Pepe brings another beer. He sets it in front of Larry. He walks away. He brings back a bottle of Espolón blanco tequila. He brings a shot glass. He sets them in front of Larry. Larry sips his beer. He pours a shot of tequila. He kills the shot.

"Thanks a lot," Larry says. "I'm gonna need this bottle."

"Help yourself!" Pepe says. "I certainly understand the feeling."

"Who's Elizabeth Charrington?" Primavera says. "We learned about you from a letter to her Alex found."

"Ah, yes," Pepe says.

He sits back down.

"Elizabeth was a lovely woman I met in New York City. She was former Spanish teacher who always enjoyed my stories about the Mexican Revolution. I continued writing to her even after I went back to Mexico and she to her hometown. She always insisted I write to her in Spanish. She wanted to keep her knowledge of the language sharp.

My heart was broken when her daughter wrote to let me know she had passed."

Alex reaches in his laptop bag. He pulls out the letter. He hands it to Pepe.

"This was in a record I bought at a store in my city."

Pepe reads the letter. He sighs.

"Elizabeth was curious about the songs we did. I was never proud enough of them to give her a copy while we were in New York. I had finally come to terms enough with them that I sent her a copy of the single. Her daughter must have sold it when she passed. It's a shame. Perhaps she needed the money, or she hated the record."

"For what it's worth, I think it's pretty good," Alex says.

He types on his laptop.

"What was working on the songs with José like?"

"A bit odd. He insisted on writing everything himself. He only let me practice the songs two or three times before recording. He usually had me play to a recording of everything else and dubbed it in later. He also had me do only one take almost every time."

"So, you don't know why he wrote about dancing in the airport?"

"I thought that was what the song was about, too. He said it was about a lover coming back from overseas."

"That makes a little more sense. Was José originally from Peru?"

"He said he was. He was in New York City to study medicine."

"Any chance you could give me his address? I'd like to get a hold of him."

"You can try."

Pepe begins writing on a piece of paper.

"You should know he doesn't like talking about his music," he says. "When I wrote and asked for a copy of the album he sent five and told me not to ask for any more."

He hands the paper to Alex.

"Thank you so much," Alex says. "Sorry I don't have more to ask, but I was trying to find the guy behind the music."

Pepe laughs.

"Don't worry, friend! I thought that might have been the case. I hope you aren't disappointed."

"Oh, no. I've got his address in Peru, so I can find him there. Thank you so much for having us."

"Thanks for the dinner," Primavera says. "It was delicious!"

Larry finishes his beer. He takes another shot of tequila.

"And thanks for the drinks. I fucking needed it," he says.

"Did you have an especially difficult trip?" Pepe says.

"Yeah, kind of," Larry says.

He takes another shot of tequila.

"'That cat you said could get me out of here?" John says. "Are they in the city?"

"No, but they aren't too far from here," Pepe says.

There is a flash of light. A face appears above the table. Larry jerks back. His chair tips over. Primavera gasps. Alex shields his eyes. Larry stands up. He rubs his head.

"Well, speak of the devil!" Pepe says. "This is Cara. They'd certainly be able to help you, John."

"We've met before," Alex says. "They helped a little, but couldn't get him out completely."

"Oh, is that so?" Pepe says. "I'm afraid if they can't help, likely no one will be able to. Cara, to what do we owe this visit?"

The face looks at Pepe. It stares at him. Pepe nods as if he can hear words. He frowns.

"Oh, dear," Pepe says.

The face disappears.

"What's going on?" Primavera says.

"There's something bad happening at the La Unión village," Pepe says. "They need my help."

"You know them?" Alex says.

"Oh, yes," Pepe says. "They're an admirable bunch. I've never joined them full-time; they're a little too idealistic for my taste. Still, I've tried to help them when I can. I assume you all met them?"

"Yes, they saved our lives," Primavera says. "Sofía was such a nice woman. Is everything okay there? They thought they were in danger and had us leave."

"Indeed, they are. I should leave for the village right away."

"How are you going to get there?" Larry says. He slurs his words. "It took us at least a day to get to here from there."

"I can get there much more quickly. Follow me. I think you all can be of help."

•

Pepe leads Larry, Alex, and Primavera to a detached garage. Alex carries the portable turntable and John. Larry carries the bottle of tequila. Pepe opens a side door. They all enter. The inside of the garage is much larger than the outside. It resembles a hangar. There is a giant tarp in the middle of the hangar. It covers what looks like a large vehicle.

"That's not what I think it is, is it?" Larry says.

Pepe grabs the tarp. He pulls it off, revealing a tank.

"You have got to be fucking kidding me," Larry says.

"Where did you get that?" Primavera says.

"I've known a lot of military folks. And a lot of former military folks. Fought beside a lot of them as well. Let's just say, I've had a lot of experience in that field and someone decided to trust me with this."

"You've had an interesting life," Alex says.

He stares at the tank. He sets the turntable on the ground. John stares at the tank.

"It's been awhile since I had to use it," Pepe says. "Come to think of it, the last time I used it, I was helping La Unión out, too. None of you know how to crew a tank, do you?"

"Fuck no," Larry says.

"Pay close attention, then. I'm going to explain everything you need to know in about ten minutes."

"Wait," Alex says. "You want us to help you with this thing?"

"Of course," Pepe says. "Your lady said La Unión saved your life. Here's your chance to pay them back."

"No. Fuck no. Fuck that," Larry says.

"Larry, drink your fucking tequila. He's right," Alex says.

Larry looks at Alex. He grumbles. He takes a snort of the tequila.

"Alex, I'm scared," Primavera says.

Alex pulls Primavera close.

"I know, baby, but look what we've been going through," Alex says. "We survived that and we'll survive this. I promise you we'll be fine. Sofía needs our help."

"You know what?" John says. "I always regretted never helping out all those cats that fought Hitler. I'm in, even if I can't do much."

"That's the spirit!" Pepe says. "Now, here's what you all need to know."

•

Larry sits in the tank's driver seat. John is next to him. Pepe sits in the commander's seat. Alex sits at the gun. Primavera sits by the ammunition compartment. Larry takes a swig of the tequila.

"Should Lobster be driving while he's drunk?" Primavera says.

"I've done it plenty of times. He seems a man that can hold his liquor," Pepe says.

"I hope so," Alex says.

"So, where are we going?" Larry says.

Pepe picks up a garage door opener sitting on the control board. He presses the button. The hangar door opens. It reveals a dark void.

"That's strange," Pepe says. "I hope we're not too late."

"What did Cara tell you was happening?" Alex says.

"That they were under attack and needed backup. They weren't very specific. We'd better hurry. Mr. Larry! Forward!"

Larry drives the tank forward. It rolls into the dark void.

The tank rolls in complete darkness. Larry looks through a periscope.

"I can't see shit," he says.

"I can't either," Pepe says. "I'm turning on the night vision."

Pepe flips a switch. The periscopes light up.

"That did it. We're almost there," Pepe says.

The tank rolls into the village. Larry stops it. Larry and Pepe look into the periscopes. The village looks deserted.

"The fuck is everyone?" Larry says.

"Everyone must be taking cover," Pepe says.

Pepe grabs a flashlight. He climbs up the hatch. He looks around. He comes back down.

"It's pitch black outside," Pepe says. "I can't see a thing. Even with the flashlight. It's like the dark is drowning out the light."

"Are we close to Sofía's house?" Primavera says.

"We're right next to it. One of us should let them know we're here."

Pepe takes a two-way radio off the wall.

"The rest of us can cover them from here while I direct them. This night vision looks like the only way we can see."

"I'll go," Alex says.

"But we don't know what's out there, Alex," Primavera says.

"I'll be all right."

"But, Alex..."

Alex hugs Primavera. He kisses her forehead.

"I promise I'll be okay. Besides, if anything is out there, you have this tank to help me."

"If anyone tries any shit on you, I'll run their ass over," Larry says.

"Thanks, Lobster," Alex says.

Pepe hands Alex the radio.

"It's to the right when you get out of the hatch," Pepe says. "I'll direct you once you get out."

Alex climbs out of the tank. He looks around. Everything is pitch black around him. He climbs off the tank. He walks to the right of the tank.

"Am I going the right way?" Alex says into the radio.

"Yes," Pepe says from the radio. "Keep heading forward. I'll let you know when you're about to get to the porch."

Alex walks forward. He hears a vehicle speeding. He hears gunshots. He turns to the direction it came from.

"What's wrong?" Pepe says.

"Did you hear that?" Alex says.

"No, what's going on?"

"Sounded like someone was doing a drive-by."

"Hurry and get into the house. It's not safe out there. Keep going the way you were going."

Alex walks into the dark. He holds his arm out. He kicks before he walks.

"You're almost there. Go a little to the left. The steps to the porch are coming up."

Alex walks into the dark. He kicks against the steps. He climbs up the steps. He walks up to the door. He feels for the knob. He knocks. Alonso opens the door. He is holding his rifle.

"¡Alex!" Alonso says, "¿Qué estás haciendo aquí?"

"Um, we're here to help." Alex says. "We have a tank and everything. It's Pepe's."

"¿Pepe? ¡Rápido, entra!"

Alonso waves Alex inside. He closes the door.

Sofía and Diego sit at the table. Diego and Sofia's rifles are on the table. Sofia sees Alex. She gets up. She walks up to Alex.

"Alex!" Sofía says. "Why are you here? How did you get here? Where are your friends?"

"Pepe brought us here," Alex says. "He and the others are outside in his tank."

"Pepe is here? Gracias a Dios. We could use his help."

"Cara called us. What's going on?"

"After you left, nothing else happened overnight. We thought we were safe. Then this darkness descended on us this morning. It's like one of the plagues called upon Egypt. Someone, we suspect the cartel who tried intimidating us before you left, has been driving through and taking shots at us. I was right to believe their American leader had the same evil powers as that Federales negotiator that destroyed my hometown. Some of our comrades have been able to fight back. Night vision goggles seem to break through the darkness, but we only have a few between us. The attackers destroyed Cara's shack. Thankfully, they aren't hurt. They've taken shelter in our cellar."

"Mr. Alex," Pepe says from the radio. "Is everything all right? How are Sofía and her boys?"

"Yeah," Alex says to the radio. "I'm talking to Sofía right now. Diego and Alonso look good, too."

"Ambrogio," Sofía says. "It's been so long."

Alex holds the radio out to Sofía. She takes it.

"It has been long time, my dear," Pepe says. "I assume you've been well since you haven't needed my help until now."

"Thank you so much for coming. We've been trapped in this darkness since this morning. A cartel is attacking us. Cara's been trying to dispel it, but they've been unable to."

"A cartel you say? I wonder they haven't moved in and attacked full force."

"I can only assume they have the same problem we do. They only have so much night vision equipment to penetrate the dark."

"Since Cara called us here, maybe we have something that can help them."

"I'll bring Alex down to see them. I hope you're right. Stay safe out there, Ambrogio."

Sofía hands the radio back to Alex.

"Ambrogio?" Alex says.

"It's the name he gave me when I met him," Sofía say "He's gone by many names throughout the years."

•

Alex and Sofía enter the cellar. A woman sits in the middle of the room. Her skin is dark black. She wears no clothes. Her body is covered in patterns with yellow body paint. She wears an African mask. There is black paint instead of holes for eyes and a mouth on the mask. Her head is down.

"Cara," Sofía says. "Have you been able to find a way to drive this darkness away?"

Cara raises her head. She nods. She looks at Alex.

Alex feels a sharp pain in his head. He grabs his temple. He hears the words "bring me the ghost in the record" in his head.

"Ow!" Alex says. "Damn."

"What's wrong, Alex?" Sofía says.

"I think Cara wants me to bring her John."

There is a loud boom outside. Alex and Sofía jump. The ground shakes beneath them.

"Pepe," Alex says into the radio. "What the fuck was that?"

"A jeep was firing at some of the houses," Pepe says. "I had Mr. Larry man the gun and fire at them. We got them."

"Your abilities on the battlefield continue to impress me, Ambrogio," Sofía says.

"Cara told me to bring John," Alex says. "I don't know why, but I think it will help with the dark."

"I hate to ask this of you, but can you come back to the tank to get him?" Pepe says. "I want to have Mr. Larry and Ms. Primavera here to man the gun in case more of them come."

Alex hears Larry, Primavera, and John's voices in the background. They object to Pepe's orders.

"Listen here," Pepe says, "you have to trust me. I have far more experience. I've fought in two wars and several skirmishes. Mr. Alex, I know it's dangerous, but please come back to the tank to retrieve John."

"All right," Alex says. "I'll be right there."

Alex walks up the stairs. Sofía follows. Cara stands up. She follows Alex and Sofía. Alex looks back at her. He stares at her a moment. He continues back up the stairs.

•

Alex climbs up the tank. He hears gunshots close by.

"Shit," he says to himself.

He clips the radio to his belt.

Primavera comes out of the hatch. She hands Alex the portable turntable. John floats above it. Alex kisses Primavera.

"Please stay safe, bebé," Primavera says.

"I will," Alex says. "I promise, and I haven't broken a promise yet."

Alex carries John back to the house.

"What's that Cara cat going to do?" John says.

"I don't know," Alex says.

"I hope I can help. Being stuck like this doesn't make me any good in fighting."

Alex arrives at the house. Sofía, Diego, Alonso, and Cara wait in the living room. Cara holds her hands out. Alex looks at John. John nods. Alex hands the turntable to Cara. Cara looks at John. John looks back at Cara.

"Yeah, that's cool," John says.

"What did they say?" Alex says.

"Cara wants to come inside the record with me," John says. "She says it might be dangerous, but if I can help, I'll take the risk."

Cara sets the turntable on the floor. She sets her hands on the record. The record stops. John disappears. Cara begins to glow. She disappears. The record glows. It flies off the turntable. It goes out the front door. Alex follows it out. Sofía, Diego, and Alonso grab their rifles. They follow Alex. The record flies into the sky. It stops. It hangs in the sky. It glows bright. The darkness evaporates.

Alex, Sofía, Diego, and Alonso look around. Down the road, a jeep approaches. It zigzags on the road. The driver is wearing night vision goggles. The driver rips the goggles off. He shouts. He turns the jeep around. Pablo sits next to him. His face is heavily bandaged. He stands up. He points a pistol at Alex. He fires. Alex ducks. The bullet misses. Sofia, Diego, and Alonso fire their rifles back. A shot hits Pablo in the chest. He drops his gun. He falls out of the jeep. He rolls on the ground. The jeep drives away.

Larry, Primavera, and Pepe climb out of the tank. They run towards Pablo. Alex and Sofía follow. Diego and Alonso run in the opposite direction. Pablo writhes on the ground. He clutches his wound. Larry stands over Pablo. He takes a swig from the tequila bottle.

"So, you're behind this, asshole?" Larry says.

"No," Pablo says. "The man who took my children, who made Alamo Azul disappear, he found me in the hospital."

Pablo coughs. He spits blood. Tears form in his eyes.

"He said if I cooperated, if I brought my men to help, he'd bring them back. I just wanted my children back."

"The man driving," Sofía says to Alex. "He was the man who tried to intimidate us while you were here. He must be the one who caused the darkness."

Pablo nods. He coughs more. Blood pours from his wound.

Diego runs up to the group.

"¡Mamá! I went up on the tallest roof we have," he says. "There are several jeeps gathered not far outside the village. The one we shot at is heading back to them."

"We need to get back in the tank," Pepe says. "If we can get a few good shots at them, we'll send them running. Alex, let the young man have the radio. He can direct our fire."

Alex hands the radio to Diego. Diego runs back to the roof.

Pablo lunges for his pistol. He grabs it. He points it at Alex. Primavera screams. Larry throws the tequila bottle at Pablo's hand. It shatters. Pablo drops the gun. Larry jumps on Pablo. He clamps his claw around Pablo's neck. Pablo's eyes bulge out. He grabs Larry's arm. He claws at it. Primavera buries her head in Alex's chest. Alex strokes her hair. Larry clamps his claw tighter. Pablo's hands go limp. His body shakes. His eyes roll in the back of his head. He stops moving. Larry keeps squeezing. He yanks his hand up. Pablo's neck rips. His head rolls away. Blood spurts from his neck stump. Larry stares at Pablo's body.

"Son of bitch," Larry says. "I had to waste that fucking tequila."

•

Larry, Alex, Primavera, and Pepe climb into the tank. They go back to their stations.

"Diego," Pepe says to the radio. "Where are the jeeps?"

Diego gives the location.

"It looks like the one we shot at is back there," he says.

Pepe tells Alex where to turn the gun. He tells Alex where to raise the gun. Alex follows Pepe's instructions.

"Load the gun!" Pepe says.

Primavera grabs a shell. She loads it.

"Fire!" Pepe says.

Alex fires the gun.

There is a short silence. There is a distant explosion. The radio comes back on.

"That hit them!" Diego says. "The ones left are starting to run away!"

Pepe tells Alex to raise the gun a little.

"Load and fire!" Pepe says.

Primavera loads another shell. Alex fires.

There is another distant explosion. The radio comes back on.

"Most of them are destroyed! The rest are still running," Diego says. "There's one coming back! ¿Qué demonios?"

Pepe tells Alex to lower the gun.

"Load up again," Pepe says.

"We should have brought more shells," Primavera says. "We only have a few left."

She loads the shell.

"There's the jeep!" Larry says.

"Lower the gun at it then fire!" Pepe says.

Alex lowers the gun. He fires. There is a flash. There is a loud boom.

"Bullseye!" Larry says. "We got the sons of bitches!"

Larry climbs out of the hatch. Alex, Primavera, and Pepe follow. They sit on the tank. There is a cloud of smoke from where the shell hit the jeep up the road. Sofía and Alonso run up to the tank.

"Thank you so much, Ambrogio," Sofía says.

"¡Muchas gracias!" Alonso says.

"You know you can call me anytime," Pepe says. "For anything you need."

He winks at Sofía.

"And to you and your friends, Alex," Sofía says. "You handle combat very well. Are you sure that we can't convince you to join us?"

"Sorry," Alex says. "We appreciate everything you did for us, but I don't think I could live my life like this."

"Me neither," Primavera says. "I'd miss my family back home. I don't like seeing people die either."

"This seems fun," Larry says. "But I got too much going on back in the U.S. too."

Alonso looks at the cloud of smoke. He points to it.

"¡Alguien viene!" he says.

Everyone turns towards the cloud of smoke. A man walks towards them. He is the driver of the jeep Pablo was in. His fists are clenched. His teeth are bared. His eyes are wide. He walks fast.

Alonso raises his rifle. He fires several shots at the man. The man falls. Alonso starts to approach him. The man stands back up. He looks different. Alonso jumps back.

"¡Dios mío!" Sofía says. "It's him! The Federales negotiator! ¡Señor Humo! The one who destroyed my hometown!"

Alonso fires more shots. Sofía raises her rifle. She fires at Señor Humo. He jerks with each shot. He keeps walking towards them.

"Back in the tank!" Pepe says.

Alex, Larry, Primavera, and Pepe climb back into the tank. They return to their seats.

"Load and fire!" Pepe says.

Primavera loads the gun. Alex fires. There is a flash and explosion as the shell hits.

"He's still coming!" Pepe says. "Load and fire again!"

There is another flash and explosion. Alex can smell the smoke.

"How is he still alive?" Pepe says. "Load and fire again!"

"We can't!" Primavera says. "We're out of shells!"

"Dammit!" Pepe says. "Everyone out!"

Pepe climbs out of the hatch. Alex, Larry, and Primavera follow. They run to Sofía and Alonso. Sofía and Alonso keep firing at Señor Humo. Their guns click empty. Señor Humo comes closer and closer. He is covered with blood and soot. His clothes are in tatters.

"We need to get out of here!" Pepe says. "That man is indestructible!"

Primavera looks up at the record in the sky.

"Hey, what's going on there?" she says.

The record trembles. It drops from the sky. It flies into Señor Humo. He stops. He screams. He shakes. He glows. Everyone shields their eyes.

Alex looks to Señor Humo. He lies smoking on the ground. Alex approaches him. He sees that Señor Humo has become a charred skeleton. The record lies on the skeleton.

Larry, Primavera, Pepe, Sofía, and Alonso approach the skeleton.

"Son of a bitch," Larry says. "Looks like John got the bastard. What the hell was his deal?"

"I can't say I know," Sofia says. "But he was an evil thing with a lot of power. I can only be thankful he's dead."

"Wait a second," Alex says.

Alex runs into Sofía's home. He picks up the portable turntable. He runs back outside. He runs up to the skeleton. He picks up the record. He places it on the turntable. He places the needle on the record's label. Static comes out of the speaker. He moves the needle around the record's label. Static still comes out. He moves the needle around the record. Music comes from the speaker.

"I think John is gone," Alex says.

His eyes tear up. Primavera hugs Alex. Alex looks up at the sky. He thinks he sees John's smiling face. He thinks he sees Cara's glowing face. They are there for a brief moment. They disappear.

"I think Cara is too," Alex says.

Alex moves the needle to the beginning of the record. Music plays.

Alex listens to John's sad crooning.

•

Alex hugs Sofía.

"I'm so sorry about your friend," she says. "I hope he's at peace now."

"I'm sorry about Cara," Alex says.

"They were very helpful to us," Sofía says. "Even up until the very end."

Sofía lets Alex go. Primavera hugs Sofía.

"I'm going to miss you," Primavera says.

"I will too," Sofía says. "If you ever come back to Mexico, please come visit us."

Sofía lets Primavera go. Pepe kisses Sofía. He hugs her.

"Call me again soon," Pepe says. "I'd like to see you again under better circumstances."

"Of course, Ambrogio," Sofía says. "I'll need to call on the phone or send a letter since Cara is gone."

"I guess we're even now," Larry says. "I probably won't be coming back to this fucking country. No offense."

"I understand," Sofía says. "This must have been difficult for you."

"Very," Larry says. "Can we go now? Without that wizard Cara's shortcut, it's going to take some time to get back to Mexico City."

"Yeah," Alex says. "No sense dragging out our goodbyes."

Larry, Alex, Primavera, and Pepe climb down the tank hatch. They wave to Sofía, Diego, Alonso, and several La Unión members as they get inside. They take their seats. Larry drives the tank forward.

"So, what are your plans now, friends?" Pepe says.

"I still need to get that interview," Alex says. "When I get back to Mexico City, I'm going to book some plane tickets to Peru. I'll try to track your old bandmate down there at the address you gave me."

"Maybe you will," Larry says. "I'll drive you and Pri to the airport, but I'm not going. Fuck that. I'm going back to the fucking States."

"If you insist," Alex says. "Pri, are you okay with going?"

"Of course," Primavera says. "I want to meet this musician too. He sounds like an interesting guy. We've come this far, anyway."

"I hope you can get something out of him," Pepe says. "He's a very private person these days."

"I hope so too," Alex says.

The sun is setting. Larry drives the tank up the road.

"I really hope the cops don't stop us," Larry says. "This would be a bitch to explain."

*Hidden Track*

Alex and Primavera sit in the back of a taxi. Alex holds his laptop bag.

"If the address is right, we'll be at José's house in a few blocks," Alex says.

"Did you hear back from Lobster yet?" Primavera says.

"Yeah. When I checked my email this morning, he said he got a phone in Mexico City. He's almost to the border now. He saw on the news that the town that disappeared is back too. He also said he's never driving me anywhere again."

Primavera laughs.

"He's missing out," she says. "Lima is beautiful. I hope he makes it back to Monk City okay."

"Me too. I hope he doesn't get stopped and have to deal with any crazy Border Patrol again."

The cab stops in front of a house.

"Estamos aquí. Setenta y tres soles, por favor," the taxi driver says.

Alex pays the driver. He and Primavera step out of the cab. They look at the house. There is a placard on the house.

"What does that say?" Alex says.

"It's advertising a room for rent," Primavera says.

Alex and Primavera walk up to the door. Alex rings the doorbell.

"I hope someone's home," he says. "There was no number listed in the phone book."

Nobody answers the door. Alex rings the doorbell again.

"Well, shit. Looks like they aren't home," Alex says.

"Maybe the doorbell doesn't work," Primavera says.

She knocks on the door. The door pushes open. No one is in the doorway. The house is dark inside. Primavera starts.

"It looks like nobody is home," Primavera says. "And they didn't shut the door tight."

Alex leans inside the doorway.

"Hello?" he says. "Is anyone there?"

Nobody answers. Alex looks at the floor. It is covered in dust.

"It doesn't look like anyone's been here for a while," Primavera says. "Are we at the right address?"

Alex reaches in his back pocket. He pulls out a piece of paper. He reads the address on the paper.

"This has to be the right place," he says. "Unless Pepe gave us the wrong address."

"Maybe he moved since Pepe last talked to him."

"It's weird there's no For Sale sign or anything. Did he just up and leave without even locking the door?"

Alex feels along the wall. He finds a light switch. He flips the switch. No lights come on. Alex flips the switch again. The lights still do not come on.

"Looks like the electricity is off," Alex says. "The place must be abandoned. Damn! Lobster warned me about this."

"I'm sorry, Alex."

"I say we go in and have a look. There's got to be a clue to where he is now."

"I don't know, Alex. This is reminding me too much of that mission."

"Well, that didn't go so badly, did it?"

Alex grins. Primavera giggles.

"We still shouldn't just go into other people's homes," she says.

"We came all the way down here, we may as well check it out. We're at a dead end to finding Y. Bhekhirst otherwise."

"All right. Let's be careful though."

Alex opens the door wider. Alex and Primavera look around the entryway.

"It looks like no one's been here for years," Alex says.

"That's really weird. The house doesn't look that old from the outside. I've got a really bad feeling."

"You can wait here if you want. It shouldn't take too long to look around."

"No, no. I'll come with. Just stay close to me."

"Of course, Pri."

Alex holds Primavera's hand. They walk into the house. They walk down the entryway. They come to a door to the right of them. Alex opens the door. There is a TV and a chair in the room. The TV is on. There is static on the screen. There is a boarded-up window on the other side. Light shines through the cracks.

"I guess the electricity is on," Alex says.

"I don't like this, Alex. Someone had to be here recently to turn that TV on. What if they're still here?"

"If they are, they're probably just a homeless person squatting. They probably aren't dangerous. You don't need to worry. Let's look around some more."

Alex and Primavera walk further down the entryway. They come into a living room. There is broken and dusty furniture in the center of the room. There are sheets of paper with writing taped to the walls. The shade on the window is down.

Alex walks up to the wall. He takes out his keychain. He shines the flashlight on the sheets of paper.

"What do those say?" Primavera says.

"It looks like a list of names," Alex says. "'J. Guzman, J. Gushman, J. Gazmen.' The page is covered with variations on the same name. This one too. 'Al Pool, Al Phool, Al Pule.' Huh. I think I remember those names from somewhere."

"From where?"

"I'm not sure. Can you raise that shade so I can see better?"

Primavera walks over to the window. She pulls the shade open. She looks out the window.

"Alex, it's raining outside," Primavera says. "It was clear just a minute ago."

Alex turns to Primavera. The window bursts open. Wind and rain blows into the room. Primavera shields her face. She struggles to push the window shut. Alex runs to the window. He helps to push it shut. He latches the window.

"Jesus Christ," Alex says.

He looks out the window.

"That doesn't look like the backyard," he says. "You were right, Pri. It's just like the mission. We'd better stay away from there."

He pulls the shade down. He leads Primavera away from the window.

"Should we leave?" Primavera says.

Alex looks back at the paper on the walls.

"Not yet. I remember where some of those names were from now," he says. "They were in the copyright records for Y. Bhekhirst's music. There were a bunch of names listed. I don't know why he put down that many when he filed, but I'm certain this was his house now. There's got to be something around here I can use to find him."

"Why don't we try that room over there?" Primavera says.

She points a door.

Alex and Primavera walk to the door. Alex puts his hand on the knob. He takes a deep breath.

"I hope this doesn't lead into oblivion," he says.

Alex opens the door. It leads to another room. Alex sighs.

"Thank god," he says.

He looks around the room. There is a desk in the corner. There are notebooks and papers on it. A box is by the desk. There is another window with the shade down. A broken guitar is in the middle of the room. A pile of small dolls is by the door.

Alex reaches down. He picks up one of the small dolls. He shines his flashlight on it.

"That's a muñeca quitapena," Primavera says.

"What's that?" Alex says.

"A worry doll. My cousin got some when she went to Mexico. You're supposed to put it under your pillow when you sleep and it takes your worries away."

"It doesn't look like it worked for whoever lived here."

Alex tosses the doll back in the pile. He walks over to the broken guitar. Primavera follows him. He kneels to look at it. He notices something next to it. He picks it up. It is a record jacket. Alex blows the dust off. He shines the flashlight on it. He looks at the cover art. It is an overexposed black and white photo of someone with long hair looking out a window from behind. He looks at the back. It is all black with white text. Side A is listed as "Your Broken Heart." Side B is listed as "Blue Moon." Underneath the title on Side B are the words "Composed by Richard Rodgers. Lyrics by Lorenz Hart."

"This looks interesting," Alex says.

"Who's the artist?"

"It doesn't say."

Alex looks inside the record jacket.

"The record isn't in it either," he says.

Alex tosses the record jacket back on the floor. He and Primavera walk over to the desk. He looks at the papers with the flashlight.

"These are flyers for Y. Bhekhirst's album," he says.

Alex hands one of the flyers to Primavera. Alex points his flashlight at it. She reads it.

"So, this really was his house," she says.

"I couldn't find anything about those when I was researching him," Alex says. "Those have got to be pretty rare."

Alex picks up a notebook. He reads through it with his flashlight.

"This looks like a book of lyrics," he says. "He must have still been working on new music before he left."

Alex looks at the broken guitar.

"I don't think it went well," he says.

Primavera grabs the box. She pulls it away from the wall. She opens it. Alex points his flashlight into it.

"There's a bunch of tapes and stuff in here," she says.

Alex reaches in the box. He pulls out a cassette. He examines it. The label reads "Y. Bhekhirst II."

"This doesn't look like his album," he says. "It's a homemade tape. Maybe he did record more music."

Alex looks at the window.

"It's probably a bad idea, but I'm going to try opening that shade," he says. "We need more light in here if we're going to look this stuff over."

Alex walks over to the window. He raises the shade. He stares out the window. He pulls down the shade. He walks back to the box. He picks up another cassette. He examines it with the flashlight.

"Is something wrong?" Primavera says. "Why'd you close the shade?"

"What?"

"That shade."

Primavera points at the window.

"You just opened and closed it," she says.

"Why would I do that? After that last window, we shouldn't mess with it."

Primavera stares at Alex.

"I'm going to try opening it," she says.

"If you want to. Just be careful."

Primavera walks over to the window. She opens the shade. She stares out the window. She closes the shade. She walks back to the box.

"What did you see?" Alex says.

"What?"

"In that window. What did you see when you opened the shade?"

"I didn't open the shade. Why would I do that after what happened with the last one?"

Alex looks at Primavera. He looks at the window.

"I think we should get out of here," Alex says.

"Yeah, let's. This place is even creepier than the mission."

"Let's take this stuff with us. We can look it over at the hotel."

"Is it okay to just take it? Aren't we stealing?"

"Given the way this place looks, I really doubt he'll be back for it."

"I hope you're right, bebé."

•

Alex and Primavera are in a hotel room. They sit on the bed. They look through the box. Primavera reads a notebook. Alex looks at a cassette. He takes it out of the case. He puts it in his Walkman. He puts on the headphones. He listens to the cassette.

"This doesn't sound like any song on the album," Alex says. "But it's definitely Y. Bhekhirst. Same voice, off-kilter playing, and everything."

"I don't remember these lyrics in the songs on the album, either," Primavera says. "Maybe he didn't record them."

Alex takes the notebook from Primavera. He reads it.

"These might be on one of the cassettes," he says. "There's a lot in here. It's going to take a while to go through."

"Hey, Alex? I'm really sorry. You came all the way down here to interview him and we never even found him."

"Don't worry about it. It's not like I'm leaving empty-handed."

"I know you really wanted that interview."

"I did, but this is almost as good. Maybe better. We're probably the only people who've heard or seen most of the things in here besides Y. Bhekhirst himself. They've got to be worth something."

Alex flips through the notebook.

"Huh, he wrote a song called 'Rainy Sunday'; just like one of John's songs," he says.

Primavera sighs.

"I really miss John," she says.

"I do too. I hope he's with his wife now. I know how much he missed her."

"Yeah. I hope so too."

Alex and Primavera look through the notebooks. They listen to the cassettes. Alex gets up. He grabs his laptop. He starts typing on it.

"Well, even without that interview, there's more than enough material to talk about here," he says.

"Alex, I know I told you this before, but you should really write a book about this trip," Primavera says. "This was an amazing experience."

"Yeah, you're right. I guess I can change some names and details. That way I can talk about everything that happened and about Y. Bhekhirst without incriminating us too much."

"I know you'll do a great job on it."

"What would I even call it? *The Search for Y. Bhekhirst* is a little too bland."

"I don't know."

Primavera looks at the cover of a book lying on the floor.

"You can call it something like *The Story of the Y.*"

*Acknowledgments*

Thank you to Garrett Cook and my fellow workshop students for their feedback.

Thank you to Miguel Ramirez for reading over the first draft and encouraging me.

Thank you to Kitten for all your support. I love you.

Thank you to Shawn Koch, William Box, Bo Hernö, Jeremy Maddux, Francis Nally and Al Stankard for beta reading the manuscript.

Special thanks to Gabino Iglesias for his edits on this book.

And a very special thanks to Bix Skahill for helping make this book what it is now.

Ben Arzate lives in Des Moines, IA. He is the author of the poetry collection *the sky is black and blue like a battered child*, published by feel bad all the time, and the short story collection *The Complete Idiot's Guide to Saying Goodbye*, published by NihilismRevised. This is his first novel. Find him online at dripdropdripdropdripdrop.blogspot.com.

www.ingramcontent.com/pod-product-compliance
Lightning Source LLC
Chambersburg PA
CBHW071002120726
47910CB00004B/1348